DEPUTY U.S. MARSHAL CARSTEN MCNEIL

A CARSTEN MCNEIL
WESTERN ADVENTURE
BOOK 2

Russell J. Atwater

Contents

Prologue
A Train Job

Arizona Territory, 1889

Floyd "Blacksnake" Whitfield looked at his pocket watch as he heard the train's whistle in the distance. From his position atop the hill, he saw the column of steam drawing closer.

"Right on time," he said, turning to face the five unscrupulous-looking men gathered around him. "Dusty, you get on that plunger and wait for my signal. Dixie, you keep an eye on things with that Sharps. Rest of you boys, ride with me. Time to get that gold."

A grizzled-looking man in a gray kepi took up a position on a cluster of rocks with a buffalo rifle. Another walked his horse down the hill. Floyd watched him dismount by a large rock sitting near the railroad track, where a plunger had been set up.

The sound of the locomotive grew louder as it approached. Floyd removed his hat and waved it at Dusty, who pressed the plunger down. Nothing happened.

"What the hell's goin' on?" Floyd said, his grip tightening on his reins. "Blow the damn track!"

He saw Dusty shrugging at the bottom of the hill.

"I got a clear shot, boss," Dixie said. "I'll take care of it."

"Hurry!" Floyd said. "I ain't losin' this payout 'cause some idiot can't work a plunger."

Dixie said nothing. He squeezed the trigger. An explosion arose on the track, prompting the gang's horses to rear. Floyd chuckled as he heard the scream of the locomotive's brakes, followed by a crash as it flew off the rails.

"That's our cue, boys!" Floyd yelled, spurring his horse down the hill and riding toward the wrecked train at a lope. His companions whooped and hollered as they followed him.

Reaching the train, Floyd brought his horse to a halt outside the express car. He drew one of his Peacemakers and fired it into the air. Screams emanated from inside the passenger cars. "Dusty, get it open," he said. "Noose and Granger, deal with the passengers. Midnight, you're with me." He watched two of his men draw their guns and walk toward the passenger cars.

As Dusty approached the express car, the door swung open. Two well-dressed men appeared and opened fire on the group. Floyd returned fire with Midnight. They breathed in the gun smoke and watched as one man tumbled from the car. He dismounted and strode over to the body, rolling it over. Floyd spat on the body as he noticed a Pinkerton badge on his coat.

"Damn Pink shot me," Dusty said as he writhed on the ground, clutching his abdomen.

"Get up, you lazy skunk," Floyd said as he grabbed Dusty's hand, pulling him to his feet. "You ain't done yet." He shoved Dusty into Midnight's arms.

Floyd stepped inside the express car to be greeted by the smell of blood and the sound of whimpering. The second Pinkerton guard lay slumped against the wall. Floyd noticed a gold tooth in his mouth. He reached inside and wrenched it out. A third guard sat hunched at the far end of the car next to the safe, clutching a shotgun.

Floyd raised his Peacemaker and shot him through the head. The whimpering stopped. "Dusty, blow that safe open," Floyd said. He watched as Midnight helped Dusty into the car.

Dusty lumbered over to the safe and produced a single stick of dynamite from his bag. Floyd watched him as he wedged the stick into the safe handle and struck a match. As he lit the fuse, he clutched his abdomen as he lumbered away. Floyd covered his ears as the stick exploded. He watched as the door creaked open. He strode over and checked inside, seeing wads of dollar bills.

"Yeehaw!" Midnight yelled as he saw the money.

"Bag it," Floyd said.

"Sure thing, boss." Midnight pulled a sack from his satchel and stuffed the wads into it. "Looks like we hit a jackpot here."

"We'll divide it when we get back to the camp," Floyd said.

***

A small cooking fire crackled in the box canyon where Floyd had set up his hideout. He poured a cup of coffee as he looked at a nearby hole in the ground. They had laid a blanket out next to the fire, piled with the wads of bills from the safe along with the many valuables taken from the passengers: purses, billfolds, watches, rings, necklaces, and even an ornate-looking fountain pen.

"Some haul, boss?" Midnight said, reaching for a watch. "How much are we gettin' each outta this?"

"Keep your hands off!" Floyd grabbed Midnight's wrist and glowered at him. "We gotta set some aside for el Presidente."

"Do we have to?" Dusty asked as he sat on a rock, wincing as he nursed his wound. "That guy always takes too much of our hauls."

The laughter and talk of the other gang members fell silent.

Floyd stood up and loomed over Dusty. "El Presidente knows 'bout some of the most lucrative hauls around," he said to his underling. "And he's keepin' the law off of our backs. If'n he wants his tribute, he gets it. In fact, you nearly cost us this when your trap didn't blow."

"It wasn't my fault!" Dusty said. Sweat poured down his forehead, and he turned pale.

"And since you complained about el Presidente takin' the lion's share," Floyd continued, "I figure we'll just split it five ways rather than six."

He drew his Peacemaker and shot Dusty in the chest. The rest of the gang stood up and backed away as he turned to face them. Dixie stayed sitting down, remaining stone-faced.

"Anyone else wanna complain 'bout their cut?" Floyd asked.

The other men shook their heads.

"Then I got nothin' else to say," Floyd said, twirling his gun back into its decorated holster.

He sat back down and lit a cigar as Noose and Granger took Dusty's body and dropped it in the pit.

"Whoever this el Presidente is," Floyd said as he took a puff from his cigar, "he's makin' this territory a real thieves' paradise."

Chapter 1
Deputy U.S. Marshal Carsten McNeil

The stagecoach rattled and jolted as it raced along the trail. As Carsten McNeil sat in one of the rough seats, he felt every bump against his arms and legs. He sat next to a pair of well-dressed men, who struck him as whiskey salesmen, and opposite a newlywed couple, who appeared to be around his age.

"Why are we speeding up?" the wife said in a tense voice, peering out of the window as her husband placed a reassuring hand on her shoulder.

Carsten noticed the husband's shoulders were hunched. He opened his mouth to speak, but he heard whooping and hollering behind them. He looked out the window, seeing little but trail dust from the team of horses pulling the stagecoach. Then he heard shots ring out. The other passengers screamed as bullets pounded the back of the coach.

"Highwaymen!" one salesman yelled as his partner buried his head between his knees. "We're being robbed!"

"Killed too, most likely!" the husband said as he clutched his wife's hand.

"Y'all remain calm now," Carsten said in a steady tone, raising his hand. "Don't give 'em a reason to hurt you. Once we stop, I'll handle this." He pulled back the lapel on his coat, showing the newlyweds the tin star on his vest. He placed a finger to his lips.

They heard a blast from the front of the coach. The shotgun messenger returning fire, Carsten surmised. More shots rang out, this time ahead of him, followed by a scream of pain. He took a deep breath.

"Whoa!" he heard the driver shout at the team while yanking on the reins. The horses whinnied in response.

"Brace yourselves!" Carsten said, "It's gonna get real bumpy in a second." He pressed back against the seat with his hands behind his head as he heard the wheels grinding.

The stagecoach lurched as it came to an abrupt halt, throwing the newlyweds out of their seats with a yelp. Carsten pulled his hat low as he extended a hand to the newlyweds.

"Throw that scattergun down here and keep your hands in the air," a voice commanded outside.

Carsten heard a clatter follow the demand as the shotgun fell to the ground. He took a deep breath as the stagecoach door flew open. A masked man appeared in the doorway, carrying a revolver. The newlyweds froze.

"All of you, out!" he yelled, pulling back the hammer with an audible click. "Keep your hands where I can see 'em and don't make no sudden movements, or I'll line your lungs with lead."

The two salesmen scurried out of the coach, nearly tripping over the husband as he helped his wife to her feet. Carsten groaned and clutched his arm.

"What's eatin' you, kid?" the robber asked as he turned to face him. "Get your hands in the sky and join the rest. Pony up!"

"It's my arm," Carsten said through gritted teeth. "Must've knocked it when you stopped us."

"My heart aches," the robber said. "Now get out. And no tricks!"

Carsten nodded, hoping the bandit hadn't seen his Remington concealed beneath his duster. The late morning sun bore down on him as he stepped outside, seeing the robber continue to wave a gun in his direction. He kept clutching his arm as he surveyed the scene. A second robber was on horseback, pointing a repeater at the driver and shotgun messenger. He noticed the shotgun messenger clutched a wounded arm.

"While my friend gets the lockbox open," the first robber said, holding a sack, "I want what's yours. Purses, billfolds, watches, rings. You name it, I want it in this sack. Now."

Carsten watched the passengers fumble through their pockets. He reached into his coat, shifting his gaze between the mounted bandit and the one with the sack who visited each passenger. He watched the man holster his gun to grab a necklace from the newlywed wife.

A third bandit emerged from behind the stagecoach with the lockbox. Carsten took a deep breath and pulled his coat back.

"Frank, look out!" the bandit with the lockbox yelled.

Carsten drew his Remington and fired a shot near the mount's hoof. The horse reared, throwing the rider from the saddle. He spun round and fired at the third bandit. The bullet struck the man's arm. He screamed as he dropped the lockbox on his foot. The robber with the sack turned to face Carsten. He reached for his gun.

Carsten cocked his own gun, shaking his head. "You must be Frank Wharton," he said as the robber raised his hands. "Which means one of you is Otis Coffey and the other's Milt Hobbs." He advanced on Frank, removing the robber's gun from its holster and tossing it to the floor.

"I know you," Frank replied, his hands trembling. "You're Quaker McNeil. You're the fella who sent English Bill to the boneyard last year. Never knew you was a lawman."

"U.S. Deputy Marshal Carsten McNeil," Carsten replied. "Y'all are under arrest for stagecoach robbery. And since one of you knows who I am, you might as well back down if you're aimin' to shoot me. The judge will look down favorably if ya surrender."

"Do as he says, boys!" Frank called out, speaking with a stutter. "I'd rather hang than get myself killed in a gunfight with Quaker McNeil."

Carsten glanced back at the man by the lockbox, who threw his gun aside. "Guess you're the brains of the bunch," he said with a grin. "Since there ain't no warrants outstandin' on any of y'all for murder, you ain't gonna hang for this. But you'll likely be spendin' a good deal of time in Yuma Territorial. It's your call. Now, if ya wouldn't mind, I'd like to match names to folks."

"That there's Otis," Frank replied, pointing to the fallen rider. "You mind if I help him?"

"And the other fella's Milt?" Carsten asked, pointing behind him.

Frank nodded.

"Guard!" Carsten called to the shotgun messenger. "How badly are you hit?"

"Just the arm, Marshal," the shotgun messenger replied. "I'll live."

"Can you keep Milt covered while I see Frank don't try nothin' untoward while helpin' Otis?"

The shotgun messenger jumped down from the seat and grabbed one of the discarded revolvers. He trained it on Milt.

Frank moved toward Otis and hauled him to his feet.

Otis winced as he stood up. "I think I messed up my back, Frank," he said through clenched teeth.

"Can you still stand?" Carsten asked.

"Just about," Otis replied, glowering at Carsten.

The sound of hooves attracted Carsten's attention. He noticed two riders approaching the stagecoach.

"More trouble?" The shotgun messenger asked.

As they drew closer, he recognized the colors of the horses as those of Blondie and Lancelot from his family's ranch. "No," Carsten replied, "We're fine. They're my kin. They must've heard the shootin' and are comin' to help."

His older brother, Morris, rode atop Blondie, with his Henry rifle stowed in the saddle ring. Their younger sister, Attie, trotted alongside on Lancelot with a Smith and Wesson Schofield sitting in a holster on her hip.

"Morris!" he called with enthusiastic tones as he continued to hold Frank and Otis at gunpoint. "Attie!"

"Carsten?" Morris called back, drawing his rifle and pointing it at Frank and Otis. "Well I'll be. Fancy seein' you in these parts since you moved to Prescott. Let me guess, catchin' stagecoach robbers in the act?"

"Well, I was plannin' on visitin' Cripple Gorge for a spell," Carsten replied. "But they happened to rob the stage I was ridin' on. I'm gonna take 'em to jail in Cripple Gorge 'fore I can arrange for them to go back to Prescott."

"If you need a hand," Morris said, "Attie and me are both ready and willin'."

"Much obliged," Carsten replied with a tip of his hat. "Keep 'em covered."

Carsten holstered his Remington. He walked over to Frank and Otis. "Can you still ride?" he asked them.

Frank nodded.

"My damn nag bolted," Otis said, "and my back hurts like a son of a gun."

"How 'bout you, Milt?" Carsten asked, looking back toward Milt.

"My foot's been crushed, ya baked possum," Milt replied with a scowl as the shotgun messenger removed the lockbox.

"Driver," Carsten said, "Otis and Milt are gonna be ridin' in the coach with me. They'll be cuffed and I'll keep them both covered. Sorry to the ladies and gentlemen who have to share the stage with them."

Carsten directed Otis and Milt to stand together and support each other. As Morris kept his rifle trained on the pair, Carsten directed Frank to mount his horse. As the bandit mounted, Carsten produced a pair of handcuffs from his pocket and cuffed Frank's hands behind his back. A whistle behind him prompted him to turn around. Attie produced a length of rope from her saddle and tossed it to Carsten. Nodding to her, he used it to tether Frank's ankles beneath the horse's torso.

"Morris, you keep Frank covered," he said as he stepped back from the horse. "Attie, you lead him and Milt's horse alongside the stage. As for this pair..." He handcuffed Otis and Milt.

The driver and shotgun messenger helped them inside the stage. Carsten followed them.

Back in the stagecoach, Carsten sat in the seat opposite the two robbers and drew his Remington. "Okay," he called through the window, "we can load up again now."

The passengers climbed onto the stagecoach. Carsten noticed the newlyweds sat in the vacant seats next to him. The two salesmen hesitated.

"Don't worry," Carsten said. "They ain't gonna bite. And if they do, I'm gonna shoot 'em."

One salesman sat in the vacant seat next to Milt, inching away from the bandit as far as the seating would allow. The second one sat on the floor between the two rows of seats, also trying to keep his distance from the prisoners as much as he could. Carsten stuck his left arm out of the window and gave Morris the thumbs up.

"We're all set!" Morris called to the driver, who replied by lashing the reins. The stagecoach lurched as it moved forward, prompting the two prisoners to wince and mumble profanity.

***

The afternoon sun bore down as the procession arrived in Cripple Gorge. Carsten relaxed as the driver opened the stagecoach door and let the passengers out. Carsten glimpsed the town jail outside. He noticed the sheriff waiting by the door, his own gun at the ready.

"This is your stop, fellas," Carsten said to Milt and Otis as the driver helped them out of the stage.

After the two robbers had disembarked, he stepped outside, keeping his gun trained on them.

"Who are these rips, then?" the sheriff asked.

"Frank Wharton, Otis Coffey, and Milt Hobbs," Carsten replied as he showed his deputy marshal's badge. "Wanted for stagecoach robbery in three counties. Caught red-handed this very mornin'. Gonna need to hold them here till I can get them taken back to Prescott."

"Fine," the sheriff said, "it's only midweek. We got plenty of free space."

"Much obliged," Carsten replied while tipping his hat to the peace officer.

"Thanks for saving us, Marshal," one of the salesman said, shaking Carsten's hand. "Not sure what would have happened if you weren't with us."

"Agreed," his partner added, handing Carsten a small bottle of whiskey. "Have this on us. You deserve a drink after that excitement."

"Much obliged," Carsten said again. "I'm gonna have to take statements from y'all 'fore you head on. In the meantime, this is actually my stop."

Chapter 2
Welcome Home

After collecting his belongings and accepting thanks from the passengers, Carsten leaned on the porch rail next to Morris and Attie, watching the stagecoach leave Cripple Gorge.

"Ridin' stage is a mite bumpy," he said. "Give me a horse any day."

"How come you didn't take Dan?" Morris said, laughing at his brother's complaint.

"I'd heard there'd been a new string of holdups lately," Carsten said, "so I figured I'd ride with the stage and make sure it got to Cripple Gorge safely, perhaps bring in the rips behind it all."

"Well, you did a bang-up job on that," Morris said, patting Carsten on the back.

"With a little help from you and Attie," Carsten replied with a grin. "Besides, I was headin' this way anyhow because I was gonna pay a visit to Fleur. Her birthday's comin' up, and I promised to be there for that." He patted his carpetbag.

"Well, you're doin' better than I am," Morris said with a laugh.

"Still haven't found nobody?" Carsten said. "That's a pity. I'm guessin' our folks are askin' you 'bout it?"

"Yup," Morris replied, bowing his head.

"Well, they're probably gonna be askin' when I'm gettin' hitched too," Carsten said. "How 'bout you, Attie? Still with Davey?"

"You betcha," Attie replied with a smile. "We're engaged now."

"Congratulations!" Carsten said while beaming. "I should make the wedding if there ain't no big felons needin' to be thrown in the calaboose 'round that time. Anyhow, I'm headin' over to Frenchie's to see Fleur. I'll catch y'all on the trail." He picked up his bag and tipped his hat.

"We'll head back," Morris said. "If'n you're lookin' for a place to stay, I can bring the buckboard. I'm sure that the rest of us will be happy to see you home. Perhaps Fleur can come back with you."

"Well, I sure would appreciate that," Carsten replied, shaking his brother's hand.

Carsten breathed in the familiar smell of floor polish as he stepped into Frenchie's General Store. He heard someone sweeping down one aisle as he noticed Hector "Frenchie" Carpentier behind the counter.

"Howdy, Marshal," he said with a combination of the French accent that earned him his moniker and hints of a southern drawl.

"Howdy, Mr. Carpentier," Carsten replied, shaking the shopkeeper's hand. "But there's no need to be callin' me, Marshal. I'm off duty. Carsten will do just fine."

The sound of sweeping stopped at the mention of his name, followed by the broom dropping with a clatter. "Carsten!" Fleur, Frenchie's daughter, cried out as she ran to the counter to see him.

"Fleur!" Carsten cried back, embracing his sweetheart, whom he'd bonded with after she helped him rescue his sister from a land baron the previous year.

"It's great to see you back in Cripple Gorge," she said. "You gonna be here long?"

"You didn't think I was gonna miss your birthday, now?" Carsten said with a wink. "In fact, I got a gift for you from Prescott." He opened his carpetbag and pulled out a small wrapped box. He handed it to Fleur.

"What is it?" she asked as she admired the box. "Mind if I open it now?"

"Well, you can for me," Carsten said as he leaned on the counter, exchanging a nod with Frenchie.

"I guess my birthday's come early, seeing you here," Fleur said. She unwrapped the box, finding a bottle of perfume.

"That's genuine Parisian lavender," Carsten said as he watched Fleur open the bottle and sniff the contents. "Paid for after bringin' in a wanted killer."

"It smells wonderful," Fleur replied with an approving nod. "Have you heard about your sister?"

"That I have," Carsten said. "Davey's a decent fella. He'll make a fine husband."

"I reckon you will too," Frenchie said, nudging Carsten.

"All in good time, Mr. Carpentier," Carsten replied. He noticed Fleur blushing. "I got a small room back in Prescott, but I'm hopin' to afford one of the nice picket-fence houses on the outskirts."

"You wanna stay over?" Frenchie asked as his daughter grinned.

"Thanks for the offer," Carsten replied, "but Morris is gonna head by with the buckboard later on and bring me back to Pa's ranch. If'n word spreads, I'm back in town, they're gonna be askin' if I'm gonna come home for a spell. I was gonna ask if Fleur wants to join us for dinner tonight? I'm sure Ma can feed a couple extra mouths. Morris has a big appetite anyhow."

Fleur giggled. "I'd love to!" she said, giving Carsten another hug.

"I reckon Morris will be back in a couple of hours," Carsten replied. "So I might hang around here till then. You folks need a hand in the store?"

"That'd be nice of you," Frenchie said. "If you ever tire of being a lawman, you'd make a crackerjack clerk."

Carsten stroked his chin as he contemplated the words. "I'm more than happy to," he said, "but first I gotta wire Marshal Cooper in Prescott and organize a wagon to take those rips to the county jail."

***

The sun was setting as Morris drove the buckboard down the trail. Carsten sat on the back beside Fleur, their arms over each other's shoulders, trying to stay in line with the bouncing of the board.

"Nice to see you got this replaced," Carsten said to his brother, thinking about the time their previous buckboard had been torched by men trying to strong-arm them into selling their ranch a year ago.

"Yeah, since the railroad came to Prescott, we've been able to find plenty of buyers for the herd," Morris replied. "Things have been pretty good 'round here now that Moraday's no longer gunnin' for nobody's land. Especially after a judge decided his company had to give us some steers to compensate for those that got burned."

Carsten turned around and saw his family's ranch coming into view. The ranch house, the barn, and the corral seemed unchanged from when he left a year ago. He noticed his father, Vince, sitting in his favorite chair by the porch, while hired hands Davey and Mike were riding toward the yard from the pasture.

"Well, I'll be," Davey said as he rode parallel to the buckboard. "It's Carsten! How the blazes are ya?"

"All the better to be seein' y'all again!" Carsten replied as Morris brought the buckboard to a halt outside the main house. "How've you been keepin'?"

"Fine as cream gravy," Davey replied as he dismounted. "Gettin' hitched to Attie real soon, if ya haven't heard already."

"I heard," Carsten replied as he shook Davey's hand. "How 'bout you, Mike? Keepin' outta trouble?"

Mike nodded in response, giving Carsten a friendly thump on the back that almost knocked him off balance.

"He's still a man of few words, as always," Davey remarked with a laugh.

"I can see that," Carsten replied.

Vince picked up his crutch from where he'd propped it up against the wall and hauled himself to his feet.

At the same time, his mother, Cassie, emerged from the house with her apron on. "Carsten!" she said as she ran out, embracing her son. "I only just heard from Morris that you were back in Cripple Gorge."

"Yes," Vince said, shaking Carsten's hand. "It's great so see you again, son. You too, Miss Carpentier."

"It's great to be back," Carsten said. "I was passin' this way on the trail of a couple road agents, and I figured I could work it into a trip to see you and Fleur."

"Well, why don't you come on in?" Cassie said, beckoning him inside the house. "Dinner's almost ready, and I made plenty for everyone."

***

Carsten hunched as he sat at the family dinner table, looking at the bowls that had been laid out, along with the two loaves of bread. While a family of five had ample space, the presence of Davey, Mike, and Fleur made things more cramped. Vince took his usual place at the head of the table, and Cassie sat to his right, opposite Morris. Carsten sat beside his older brother, opposite Fleur. Davey sat beside him, opposite Attie, while Mike sat at the far end. They had borrowed stools and chairs from the dresser tables in the bedrooms.

"So, how's workin' as a lawman?" Vince asked Carsten as Cassie doled out ladles full of beef stew into the bowls.

"Keeps me busy," Carsten said, nodding to his mother as she filled his bowl with stew. "Most of it's getting statements from witnesses and giving evidence in court."

"You said you were on the trail of three road agents?" Vince said.

"Caught 'em," Carsten said with a nod. "They held up the stagecoach I happened to be ridin' on."

"You take 'em alive?" Vince asked.

"Yep," Carsten replied. "One fella messed up his back fallin' off of his horse, and another fella got his foot crushed after he dropped the lockbox on it. That kinda persuaded the third to back down. I'm surprised Morris or Attie hadn't told you 'bout it. They happened to be ridin' by and came to help."

"We wanted you to tell it," Attie said. "You're the hero of the hour, after all."

An uproar of laughter arose from everyone. Carsten picked up his spoon and prepared to tuck into the stew.

"Carsten McNeil, aren't you forgetting something?" Cassie said.

He looked up and saw his mother staring him down while everyone else bowed their heads. "Sorry Ma," he said with an uncomfortable laugh. "I keep forgettin' things like that when I'm on the trail." He put down his spoon, bowing his head and clasping his hands together.

"Come, Lord Jesus, be our guest," Vince said, "and bless what you have bestowed. Amen."

"Amen," Carsten said in unison with everyone else. He tore up a piece of bread and dropped it into the stew.

"Whereabouts you stayin' in Prescott?" Davey asked.

"I got me a room in the Granite Mountain Hotel," Carsten replied before chewing on a mouthful of beef. "But I'm hopin' to move into one of them quaint little houses on the outskirts. Just gotta find some high-payin' felon."

"How long are you planning to stay here?" Cassie asked.

"Reckon it'll just be one night," Carsten replied. "Tomorrow I need to head back to Prescott with them road agents I got waitin' in the town jail. There's a wagon arrivin' tomorrow."

"I need to pick up supplies," Cassie said, "so I'll take you and Fleur back in the buckboard."

"Much obliged," Carsten said.

***

As night fell, Carsten leaned on the porch rail and watched the stars. He heard the familiar tapping of his father's crutch on the decking behind him.

"What's eatin' you, son?" Vince said as he leaned on the porch rail beside him.

"Just thinkin' 'bout life," Carsten said.

"I've been hearin' all kinds of stories of you bringin' in the road agents in this county," Vince said. "In the space of a year, you've become a better lawman than I ever was. I couldn't be prouder of you." He patted Carsten on the shoulder.

"Thanks, Pa," Carsten replied. "I always figured it was gonna be tough when I got that label, Quaker McNeil. I've occasionally had a dangerous gunfighter who I had to gun down when they wanted to challenge me, but that probably stuck things for most folk."

"Sometimes violence perceived is violence achieved," Vince said. "Your reputation can serve you well, but one day it's gonna work against you. I don't know how, but there's always gonna be some rip who's as cunnin' as a fox who'll be able to tear apart that reputation you built up."

"I guess I'll have to keep watch for that day, if'n it ever comes," Carsten said.

A silence followed as both men watched the stars.

"Anyhow," Vince said as he picked up his crutch, "I'd best go to bed. I'm sorry it's gonna be a mite crowded."

"I've slept in tighter places," Carsten replied. "But I might stay out here a little while longer. G'night, Pa." As Vince hobbled back inside the house, Carsten stroked his chin. "Perhaps another storm is gonna be comin' in real soon," he said to himself.

Chapter 3
Duty Calls

Carsten saw the prison wagon in front of the sheriff's office before the buckboard even reached Cripple Gorge's main street. As he sat beside Fleur and Cassie, he noticed the various townspeople looking at the wagon and the drab-looking deputy marshall at the reins, dressed in all black and reading what he deduced to be a small Bible. He put the book down and stared at Carsten as the buckboard approached.

"Will you excuse us?" Carsten said, handing the reins to his mother. "I reckon I'm gonna be ridin' back with them." He embraced Cassie and Fleur.

"Be careful," Fleur said. "Hope you can come back soon."

Carsten dismounted and strolled toward the wagon. "Morning," he said as he approached.

"You're late," the deputy said.

"Well, that can't be helped now, can it?" Carsten replied. "Come on, let's get those bandits loaded up."

The deputy picked up a shotgun resting on the seat beside him and dismounted.

"My handle's Carsten McNeil, by the by." He extended his hand.

"Nash," his companion replied. "Pete Nash." He walked into the sheriff's office without returning the handshake or making eye contact.

"You must be based in Phoenix," Carsten said. "I ain't seen you in these parts."

Nash ignored him.

Carsten stepped inside the sheriff's office, seeing the three road agents in the two cells. Otis lay on the cot in the first cell, while Frank sat hunched against the wall. Milt lay on the cot in the other cell, his arm bandaged and his leg in a splint.

"U.S. Deputy Marshals McNeil and Nash," Carsten said. "We're takin' these fellas back to Prescott."

"All of you…" Nash pointed the shotgun at the prisoners. "Up and out."

"Easy," Carsten said. "Two of them have trouble walkin'."

Nash ignored the remark. He thumbed back the hammers on the shotgun.

Frank moved to help Milt up.

"You boys had best do as my partner says," Carsten said. "He's a mite jumpy and not the most sociable fella."

"You headin' back too?" the sheriff asked Carsten as he moved to unlock the gate.

"He is," Nash replied. "Marshal Cooper's waitin'."

"He's back in Prescott?" Carsten said. "This must be serious."

"Duty calls," Nash said. His gaze remained on Frank and Otis as they staggered out of the cell. He led them out of the door to the marshal's office.

"Deputy, you help Milt," Carsten said. He stepped outside and opened the wagon door.

Nash ushered Frank and Otis into the back, slamming the door shut as they entered. Carsten locked it.

"Get the other one," Nash said.

Carsten stepped back toward the sheriff's office. The sheriff stepped outside with Milt, who limped along. Carsten unlocked the gate as Nash aimed the shotgun inside the wagon.

"In," Nash said.

The sheriff helped Milt inside the wagon.

Frank moved forward to assist them.

"Back!" Nash screamed, pulling back the hammers on both barrels.

Frank raised his hands and stepped away from the door.

"There ain't no call to be threatenin' the prisoners like that," Carsten said. "One's got a messed up back, and another's got a broken foot."

Nash said nothing, watching as Milt struggled to climb into the wagon. Once the road agent got inside, the deputy slammed the gate shut and locked it, handing the keys over to Carsten. "Take the reins," he said.

Carsten nodded, clambering up to the driver's seat. Nash sat beside him, gripping the shotgun. Taking a breath, Carsten flicked the reins, and the wagon rolled forward. He nodded to the passersby as they stepped back to allow the wagon to pass.

***

As the late morning sun shone over the trail, Carsten looked ahead. He spotted a group of ranch hands driving a trail in the distance. "You been a marshal long?" Carsten asked Nash.

His partner remained silent.

"I couldn't help but notice that Bible you got there," Carsten continued. "Are you some kind of lay preacher?"

Silence.

"Definitely an antisocial type," Frank piped up from within the cage.

"Quiet!" Nash snapped.

"Yes, sir," Frank replied with a sarcastic tone.

"How are Milt and Otis doin'?" Carsten asked Frank.

"Not good," Frank replied. "The bumpiness of this trail ain't doin' no favors for Otis. And the cage is gettin' real hot."

"No talking to the prisoners," Nash said.

"Now wait just a minute," Carsten replied. "I already told you two of them were injured. And maybe they need water."

"Suffering is good for the soul," Nash said.

Carsten shuddered. He reached into his pocket and produced the small bottle of whiskey he'd been given as a gift by one of the stagecoach passengers.

"Hey, Frank," Carsten called out. "You boys want a drink on me?"

"I wouldn't say no to a splash of whiskey to take the edge off things," Frank replied. "Thanks, Carsten. You ain't so bad for a lawman."

"No!" Nash snatched the bottle from Carsten and threw it away. "I won't allow the sharing of the demon drink."

"Hey," Carsten said. "There was no call for that either."

"It's sinful," Nash said, glowering at Carsten. "I suppose you fornicate with harlots, too?"

"Mister," Carsten said, "I like a good drink every once in a while, always when I ain't workin'. I don't do not need to go after your so-called harlots when I'm already courtin' the girl of my dreams. And I still make the time for Sunday church when the circuit preacher's in town. And I ain't gonna get in the way of no workin' fellas wants unless they're itchin' to kill somebody. But I ain't in church right now, and I don't need no sermon."

"Yeah, and I'll plead guilty if I don't have to be guarded by this sour fella," Frank said.

Carsten laughed at the prisoner's remark as Nash aimed him a murderous glare. He took a breath.

***

The early afternoon sun set as the prison wagon rolled into Prescott. Carsten felt his shirt sticking to him. He wiped the sweat from his brow as he brought the team of horses to a halt outside the county jail. He noticed a grizzled-looking man with a bushy walrus mustache standing by the entrance. He recognized him as Rufus Horne, the sheriff of Yavapai County and an old friend of his father. Two guards with shotguns flanked the sheriff.

"Howdy, Rufus," Carsten said, tipping his hat.

"Carsten," Rufus said with a nod, "good to see you made it back."

"Much obliged," Carsten replied. "We'll get these boys in the cells first." He unlocked the wagon as Nash aimed the shotgun inside.

"End of the line, boys," Carsten said. "Come on out."

Frank helped Otis and Milt out of the wagon. Two guards led them away.

"Marshal Cooper's waitin' in the office," Rufus said as he followed the guards. "He's askin' for you and Nash."

"I'll be right there," Carsten said. "You joinin' us?"

"Nope," Rufus said. "He said it's a federal matter, not a county one. Reckon it's somethin' to do with that train robbery happened a couple of weeks back. But that was in Maricopa, and I got no jurisdiction there."

"Well, you have a good day now," Carsten said, shaking Rufus's hand. The sound of Nash clearing his throat prompted him to turn toward the door. "Duty calls," he said, rolling his eyes.

Carsten and Nash walked inside the jailhouse and stopped by a closed door. Carsten knocked.

"Who is it?" a voice inside called out.

"Deputies McNeil and Nash," Carsten replied.

"Come in."

Carsten and Nash stepped inside the office. The blinds were closed, which did little to alleviate the sticky heat.

U.S. Marshal Ross Cooper, a rugged-looking man with a patch over his eye, sat behind a desk with a folded newspaper. "Sit down, fellas," he said, gesturing to the vacant chairs in front of the desk. "Bang-up job bringin' in those road agents, by the way."

"Thank you, sir," Carsten replied as he sat down.

"We'll see how it plays out when it goes to trial," Ross said. "I see you've met Deputy Marshal Pete Nash."

"Yeah..." Carsten said. "He stationed in Phoenix?"

"Yup," Ross said. "He's a mite fanatical 'bout things, but he's a dedicated lawman. Anyhow, to business. You might have heard 'bout this train robbery down in Maricopa?"

"I heard," Carsten said. "The sheriff was talkin' 'bout that just now."

"Well, this'll fill you in." Ross handed an issue of the *Phoenix Herald* to Carsten.

He unfolded it and looked at the front-page story. "Three dead in Desert Flyer robbery," Carsten read aloud. "The Desert Flyer was the latest target in a string of stagecoach and train robberies that have been plaguing the Arizona Territory in the past month. A gang of five riders derailed the train by dynamiting the track. Two of them entered the passenger cars and robbed everybody present, while the other three stormed the express car and killed three Pinkerton guards assigned to protect it before making off with the contents of the safe. Mr. Alden of the railroad has offered a reward of one thousand dollars for the capture of the ringleaders of these gangs, and an additional four hundred dollars for any of their accomplices, dead or alive."

"It induces sinful greed," Nash said.

"Is everything sinful to this fella?" Carsten asked Ross.

"Your smart remarks likely will be," the marshal replied, "but he's right. The railroad's reward has stirred up a real hornet's nest. We've had would-be gunfighters comin' back as freight, sometimes in several boxes. We've got feudin' families using the robberies as an opportunity to exchange lead with each other. And we've got a lot of local toughs usin' the scheme as an excuse to shoot Indians or Mexicans throughout the territory."

"That ain't good," Carsten said. "So what's the plan?"

"I need you to come back to Phoenix with me," Ross said. "I'm puttin' a posse together to try to keep the freelancers in check. I already spoke to the railroad and made sure anyone who wants to qualify has to be sworn in. Are you good to join me?"

"I reckon so," Carsten said. "We leavin' now?"

"The next train to Phoenix is tomorrow morning at eight o'clock," Ross said. "That'll give you time to get supplies together and write a letter to your sweetheart."

"Tomorrow at eight," Carsten said as he stood up. "I'll be there."

***

As night fell, Carsten sat hunched at the desk in his room at the Granite Mountain Hotel. He fidgeted with a pencil as he stared at the sheet of paper in front of him, blank except for the hotel's letterhead.

"My dearest Fleur," he said aloud. "Hmm... maybe not."

He tapped the desk with the blunt end of the pencil.

"Dear Fleur," he said as he wrote it down. "I trust this letter finds you well. They have called me to Phoenix to serve on a federal posse, going after some train robbers. I don't know how long I'll be gone for, but I hope to see you again once I do my work in the territory's new capital. There's a big reward out for these people, and I hope things won't get too competitive out there. If all goes well, I might look at one of those houses in Prescott I was telling you about. We'll have a lot to talk about soon. I can't wait to see you again. Yours with love, Carsten."

He smiled to himself as he signed the letter, folding it in an envelope. He set it aside and opened the desk drawer where he'd kept the Colt Frontier he carried as a backup to his Remington.

Chapter 4
A County Matter

The following morning, Carsten stood on the station platform with Ross and Nash. He heard a clock in the distance ring eight times and stared down the track.

"How's the family, Carsten?" Ross asked.

"They're doin' good, sir," Carsten replied. "Morris has been tendin' the ranch well, with Davey and Mike's help. In fact, Attie's gettin' hitched to Davey real soon."

"That's real good," Ross said. "How 'bout you? How's things with the lovely Miss Fleur?"

"Things are good," Carsten replied. "I sent her a letter 'fore I came here. I reckon she's gonna miss me somethin' fierce while we're down in Phoenix."

"Well, it's always good to have someone to look forward to seein' back home," Ross said, patting Carsten on the back. "You should spend plenty of time with her while you're still young."

"I'm thinkin' of proposin' once I get back from this little jaunt," Carsten said. "If'n this job pays handsome, I might invest in a new home in Prescott. We could build a new life together."

"You do that," Ross said with a grin. "I often wish I'd spent more time with my wife when I was closer to your age. Before the yellow fever took her."

"I'm sorry," Carsten said, removing his hat and holding it to his chest.

"Don't be," the marshal replied. "It's been almost fifteen years now."

Carsten opened his mouth to speak, but the sound of a train whistle interrupted him.

As the train pulled into the station, the smell of the boiler greeted Carsten. He followed Ross and Nash into one of the passenger cars. He sat down on the hard wooden seat opposite the pair.

"Reckon it's gonna be around four hours to get to Prescott," Ross said. "You'd best get some rest while you still can."

Carsten nodded in agreement. He leaned back in his seat and pulled his hat over his eyes.

***

Carsten woke up, sweating, as he felt a boot in his leg. The heat of the midday sun, combined with the steam from the locomotive, made the passenger car feel like a sauna. He removed his hat and mopped the sweat from his brow. Through the window, he noticed a woman in a wide-brimmed hat and duster standing at the platform and carrying a Winchester.

"We're here," Nash said. The train jerked to a halt as he finished speaking.

Carsten stood up, tipping his hat to a lady as she made her way down the aisle. He stepped off the train.

The woman with the rifle approached the marshal. "I hear you're the man to see regarding hunting some train robbers," she said with a strong Mexican accent.

"That's right," the marshal replied. "U.S. Marshal Ross Cooper. These here are my deputies, Carsten McNeil and Pete Nash."

"Ramona Vasquez," the woman replied.

"I heard of you," Ross said. "Fellas, this here's one of the meanest bounty hunters in the territories. The kind of person we want ridin' with us."

"Pleasure to make your acquaintance," Carsten said, extending his hand.

She ignored the offer of a handshake. "I've heard about you, Quaker McNeil," she said. "Your reluctance to kill won't serve you well here."

"Why don't you get your horses," Ross said. "I'll meet you at my office."

Carsten made his way to the nearby yard. Two stable hands unloaded horses from the train's livery car. He noticed Dan, his chestnut gelding, being offloaded. He checked the Winchester rifle he kept in a saddle ring. His roan pack horse, Bill, followed close behind. He tipped his hat to the stable hands and led them away.

Marshal Cooper's office in Phoenix was a short walk from the station. Carsten led Dan and Bill to the office and hitched them outside. Ross stood in the doorway, flanked by Nash and Ramona. Three other gunmen had gathered in front of the building.

"Are these fellas ridin' with us, too?" Carsten asked as he looked them over.

"That's right," Ross said. "Charlie, Ike, and Buford. Boys, this here's my deputy, Carsten McNeil."

Carsten nodded as he shook their hands. "You folks lawmen or freelancers?" he asked.

"I'm normally a shotgun messenger for the stagecoaches," Charlie said. "Ike's a bouncer at the saloon. Buford's a cowhand used to fightin' money. We've all ridden together in posses before."

"Well, anybody who knows the workings of a shootin' iron can be tied to," Carsten said. "As long as y'all can keep level heads and not start shootin' wild."

The sound of a man clearing his throat prompted Carsten to turn around. He noticed another man approaching, dressed in a gray tailored suit and derby hat and carrying an ornate walking stick. He stood near the marshal with a look of disdain. "So, this is your posse, Marshal Cooper?" he said as he viewed the members of the posse.

"Carsten," Ross said, "I'd like you to meet John Garrett, the sheriff of Maricopa County."

"Carsten McNeil?" Garrett said as he extended his hand. "Ain't you the fella who killed English Bill? I'd say you're gonna be a fish outta water down here with your Quaker leanings."

Carsten's lips pursed as he shook the man's hand. "I ain't no Quaker," Carsten replied. "Folks started callin' me Quaker McNeil through a fluke that arose from my first gunfight. You know how tall yarns spread 'round these parts, don't ya?"

"Your boy's modest," Garrett said to Ross. "That's good. I ain't got no time for braggarts. When I first laid eyes on him,

I thought he was gonna be some boastful young buck who's all gurgle and no guts." He gave Carsten a slimy grin.

"I get that a lot," Carsten said. "And frankly, when I laid eyes on you, I mistook you for a tinhorn."

The smile on Garrett's face died down.

Carsten saw Ross glare at him, but noticed a faint smile come to his lips. "So, are you joinin' us on this hunt?" Carsten asked the sheriff. "I figure we could work together in catchin' these rips."

"I appreciate the offer," Garrett said, "but frankly, I'd like to keep this a county matter."

"If it's a county matter," Carsten replied, "why haven't you raised your own posse?"

"Because I've been dealing with many incidents that arose since Alden posted that reward," Garrett said, fidgeting with the top of his walking stick.

"Don't federal matters trump county matters?" Carsten asked.

"They do," Ross stared at Garrett. "I want suspects. I want outstanding warrants. And I want 'em now."

Garrett slammed his walking stick on the ground. He produced a folded sheet from his pocket and handed it to Ross. Carsten peered over as Ross unfolded the sheet, revealing it to be a wanted poster. He noticed a distinct scar that ran across the man's face.

"The handsome fella in the picture's Wiley Frye," the sheriff said. "Wanted in connection with three stagecoach robberies and one bank robbery. Last seen in Gold Canyon. That's in Pinal County and out of my jurisdiction. Perhaps you can go after him. After all, it's a federal matter."

Carsten saw the marshal's fist tighten.

"Fine," Ross said. "We'll go after Frye."

"Good luck!" Garrett said. He smiled and patted the marshal on the arm before walking away.

"How in the hell did that fella get made a sheriff?" Carsten said as he watched him leave. "He looks like he's never forked a bale of hay in his life."

"Town's gettin' civilized," Ross said, spitting a wad of tobacco juice on the floor beside him. "He's probably got connections, so all the shopkeepers vote him in. And as a sheriff, he also collects the taxes. Probably takes more than his fair share. I hear he's got a fancy hacienda outside of town."

"Wish I could afford a place like that," Carsten said as he rolled his eyes.

"Same here, kid," Ross said, patting him on the shoulder. "But Wiley Frye has a warrant outstandin'. So let's mount up!"

Carsten nodded in agreement. He mounted Dan, watching the other posse members as they followed the marshal out. Carsten clicked his tongue and rode Dan out in a trot while Bill trailed behind, tethered to the riding horse with a length of rawhide.

Chapter 5
Unfinished Business

Two weeks earlier

The staccato of hammers on stone resounded through the yard of Yuma Territorial Prison. Tucker swung his hammer, trying to steal glances around the yard with the other inmates as they broke rocks. He kept his head bowed as the guards trotted past.

"Keep your gaze on that hammer!" one guard shouted to another inmate.

Tucker sighed and continued to break the rocks in front of him. Sweat poured down his face and soaked through his striped uniform as the midday sun bore down on him. The sun heated the manacles on his legs, which seared his ankles. He exchanged a glance with his friend McElroy. He heard a crumpled thud as the man next to him collapsed.

"Get that fellow some water!" an inmate shouted. He put down his hammer and kneeled down to check the man.

"Quiet!" a guard replied, striking the inmate in the back with the butt of his rifle. "Someone get that man outta here."

Two other inmates moved and grabbed the unconscious man, dragging him away.

***

As night fell, Tucker lay on his bed and stared at the ceiling. The foul smell of the waste bucket festered in the heat, causing him to gag at the stench.

McElroy sat on the neighboring bed and fidgeted. "I heard tell the McNeil boy's a lawman now," he said. "I spoke to a newcomer he'd sent this way."

"What kind of lawman?" Tucker said, continuing to stare at the ceiling.

"U.S. Deputy Marshal," McElroy replied. "A lot of folks have heard of him. Got a reputation for bringin' folks in alive. Half of them surrendered to him without even tryin' to throw down. That's why they're callin' him Quaker McNeil."

Tucker's fist tightened at the remark. "Well, you were the one who refused to face him," he said. "Your reputation as a yellow belly is solid now."

"Tucker, why the hell are we here anyhow?" McElroy asked. "Surely there was someone else to pin it on? Like Big Al or English Bill?"

"They ain't breathin'," Tucker replied. "Carsten sent them both to perdition. We're still breathin', so we got blamed. I reckon we got unfinished business with that family."

"I reckon so," McElroy said, cracking his knuckles. "How do we get outta here?"

"We put on a show for the turnkeys in the mornin'," Tucker replied. He smiled as he lay back and closed his eyes.

***

The morning sun's rays shone through the bars in Tucker and McElroy's cell. Tucker groaned as he heard the rattling of keys. He climbed out of bed as the jailer opened the cell.

"Get up and ready, boys!" the jailer shouted, knocking a club against the bars on the door. "Time to get your morning vittles."

Tucker and McElroy followed the procession of inmates to the mess hall. A cook waited at a counter by the door, stirring a pot of gruel and dropping a ladleful into bowls, which he handed to the inmates.

"Tarnation," Tucker said as the smell of the gruel made his eyes water. "Am I supposed to eat this or use it to caulk a wagon?"

"You don't like it, you can starve," the cook snapped. He snatched the bowl away and hit Tucker on the head with his ladle.

"That told him," McElroy said, laughing as the cook served him his gruel.

"You'd best back down, runt," Tucker growled. "If you don't, you'll be eatin' them words."

"I ain't backin' down from nothin'!" McElroy replied. "You had the smart mouth and look at what that cost you."

"I know you," Tucker said. "You don't wanna back down 'cause folks here know you're yellow!"

The chatter of the nearby inmates fell silent.

"Say that again, you dirty scum," McElroy said in a low tone.

"I will," Tucker said, striding up to him and staring into his face. "You're a coward who refused a challenge from Quaker McNeil. And you'll be branded a coward for the rest of your days. There ain't a thing you can do to change folks' minds 'bout that."

"Well, cowards don't eat," McElroy said, "so you can have my gruel." He threw the bowl into Tucker's face, prompting an uproar from the inmates.

Tucker let out an angry yell. He grabbed McElroy and threw him into the cook's table. Bowls and spoons scattered while the cook took hold of the gruel pot and moved it out of the way. Inmates cheered as McElroy shoved Tucker back.

"What the hell's going on here?" a commanding voice yelled.

Tucker raised his head, fist pausing before it could crash down on McElroy again. A truncheon struck him across the face. He spat blood and broken teeth as he looked up, the guard standing over him with an angry look on his face.

"Complaints 'bout the cooking!" McElroy shouted. He snatched the gruel pot from the cook and dumped it on the guard's head.

A louder cheer arose from the onlookers.

Tucker stood up and punched the guard in the stomach. He saw more guards rushing to the scene. He removed the pot and wrapped his arm around the guard's neck. "Stay back!" he shouted. "Or I'll snap his neck!"

He watched McElroy remove the revolver from the guard's holster and aim it at the approaching reinforcements. The inmates surged forward, pouncing on the incoming guards.

"Come on," Tucker said to McElroy. "We're gettin' outta here."

"You ain't gonna get far," the hostage said. "The guards in the towers will shoot on sight."

"You worry 'bout your own hide," Tucker hissed in his ear. "I don't particularly like holdin' you on account of you covered in that reekin' gruel. But you got the keys, and we want outta this hellhole."

He led the guard out of the mess hall toward the gates. A rabble of inmates stormed out after them. Shots rang out from the guard towers. Tucker saw an inmate drop to the ground. Shots were fired around him as inmates with commandeered guns returned fire. He clamped a hand over the hostage's mouth and dipped into the cell blocks as more guards charged forward. Tucker saw them clash with the rioting inmates and noticed a path leading to the front gates.

"We're gonna mosey to the gates," he said to the guard. "Make any noise, and I'll wring your neck like a chicken."

"He means it," McElroy added. He jammed the barrel of the stolen revolver into the guard's back and cocked it.

Tucker and McElroy made their way along the walls toward the gatehouse with the guard. Four guards aimed repeaters at them.

"I'd drop those guns if you value this fella's life," Tucker said.

"Do as he says!" his hostage spluttered out.

The men's rifles fell to the ground with a clatter.

"Wise move," McElroy said. "Now, you'd best open the gates and let us leave."

Two of the guards nodded and moved to open the gates. A covered wagon sat outside, being unloaded by two freighters.

"That looks like our ride outta here," Tucker said, nodding to McElroy.

His companion climbed into the driver's seat and lashed the horses.

"Hey!" one freighter yelled as the wagon moved.

Tucker threw the guard into them and ran to the wagon, jumping into the back. Seeing a freighter inside, he punched the man in the face, knocking him out. As shots echoed from the towers, he noticed the Colt Army in a holster on the unconscious man's gun belt.

"Hey, Tucker!" McElroy called from the driver's seat. "What's that fella wearin'? I could use some new duds."

"He's about your size," Tucker replied. He removed the man's clothes and dumped him over the back of the wagon.

"We're away!" McElroy said, cackling. "Those turnkeys will be too busy dealin' with the riot to chase us."

"Let's hope," Tucker said as he rummaged through the pockets of the stolen clothes, admiring a watch.

"Where we headin'?" McElroy asked.

"We'll follow the Gila River to Phoenix," Tucker replied. "That'll take us to Agua Caliente in five days' time."

***

As the sun set, Tucker and McElroy brought the wagon to a halt near the banks of the Gila River.

Tucker unhitched the team of horses from the wagon, slapping two of them so they bolted into the distance. "That oughtta throw 'em off our trail," he said, noticing a column of smoke rising ahead of them.

McElroy opened his mouth to speak, but Tucker hushed him.

"There might be some folks nearby," he whispered. "You check 'em out. See if they're friendly."

"Why me?" McElroy asked.

"Well, you're dressed for it," Tucker replied, tugging the striped shirt they had issued him at the prison.

"Fine," McElroy said. He skulked away.

Tucker stooped by the river and splashed water on his face before returning to the shade provided by the wagon. He heard a gunshot in the direction McElroy had gone, prompting him to grab the Colt Army he'd stolen from the freighter. Cocking it, he approached the column of smoke.

As he drew closer, Tucker noticed a small campsite by the river. Someone had made a cooking fire outside a small one-man tent. A hobbled pack mule sat nearby. McElroy sat by the cooking fire, helping himself to a plate of beans. The campsite's burly occupant lay still beside him. As Tucker drew closer, he saw the man's rugged attire. He noticed a bullet hole in the man's forehead.

"He ain't friendly," McElroy said, his words muffled by a mouthful of beans. "Glad you're here. That prospector's a big bastard. Need help dumpin' him in the river."

Tucker looked at the body. "Well, it's a cut above what I'm wearin' right now," he said, and removed the dead man's clothes.

"He's got some supplies on the pack mule we could use," McElroy said. "Only one bowl, though. But I found this." He picked up the bottle of whiskey that lay by his feet and took a swig.

"You'd best fetch them horses," Tucker said. "We'll bring them here."

"Damn it," McElroy said as he stood up. "I'd just made myself comfortable."

"Jump to it," Tucker said. "I'm hungry, and I need to change what I'm wearin'."

As McElroy walked past, Tucker snatched the whiskey from his hand. He took a swig and helped himself to the beans in the pot.

When McElroy returned to the campsite with the two remaining horses, Tucker had changed into the dead prospector's overalls and dumped the body in the river.

"So," McElroy said, "where do we go from here?"

"We'll keep followin' the river to the nearest town," Tucker replied. "Then I reckon we pay a visit to the McNeil family in Cripple Gorge."

Chapter 6
Trailing Wiley Frye

Present day

The afternoon sun bore down as Marshal Cooper's posse rode the trail from Phoenix toward Gold Canyon. Carsten maintained Dan and Bill's trot as he looked toward the foothills and mesas of the Superstition Mountains, which appeared small in the distance. He watched as Ramona led the posse along the route, taking point.

"You know much 'bout Ramona?" he asked Ross as he rode parallel to him.

"Only by her reputation," Ross said. "I once heard she walked into a saloon where a trio of liquored up rips were bullyin' some tinhorn. When they saw her, they picked a fight. Beat two of them so bad they can only take soup to this day."

"What happened to the third guy?" Carsten asked as his eyes widened.

"He had a genius notion of skinnin' his smoke wagon," Ross said as he lit a stogie. "She sent him to the bone orchard. And the fella they were pickin' on turned out to be some banker wanted for stealin' from his own bank, so she turned him in."

"Sounds like she's gonna be someone to ride the river with on this venture," Carsten remarked.

"I reckon so," Ross said. "First time I met her, she'd ridden into one town and shot the sheriff. Turned out the fella was a wanted rustler who'd been livin' under a false name. When I tried to bring her in, she just stepped outside with the handbill, askin' for the reward."

"Well, I hope she don't shoot Wiley like that," Carsten said. "I'd prefer to bring him in alive."

"So would I," Ross said, "but you know these bounty huntin' types. Posters say dead or alive, and the dead don't complain 'bout the journey back. Guess we'll see what happens."

***

As the sun began to set, the posse set up a campsite near the outskirts of Mesa. Carsten brushed down his horses and watched as the other members tended to their own horses, set up bedrolls, or made a fire.

"Why can't we stay in town?" Buford asked as he stoked the fire. "We could sleep in proper beds, get some decent grub, and maybe find some place for a card game. Or find some girls."

"That's sinful," Nash said, pointing at the trail hand. "You will face eternal damnation for your life of vice."

"Well, I'm guessin' that decision was to appease Mr. Fire and Brimstone there," Carsten said.

As Buford let out a hearty laugh at the remark, Nash aimed a glare at Carsten before skulking away.

"I'm sorry for the budget trip," Ross said as he approached the campfire, "but I couldn't convince Mr. Alden from the railroad to cover our expenses. They're just payin' for whoever we bring in. On top of that, I ain't riskin' big boots and loose lips leadin' back to Wiley and his boys."

"How many folks you reckon he's got?" Charlie asked, looking up from cleaning his shotgun.

"Most of Wiley's gang operate in fours," Ross said. "But I reckon he has at least a dozen men at his beck and call. He's probably got some of his boys in many towns 'round these parts, and they're likely to have ears to the ground. He's a real popular figure."

"All the more reason to avoid the towns," Carsten said as he tore a chunk of jerky with his teeth.

"Pretty much," Ross said. He gave Carsten a proud smile.

"Where do you reckon he's hidin'?" Carsten asked.

"There're caves in the mountains," Ramona said. "Plenty of places for him to hide."

Carsten turned his head and noticed her seated away from the fire and staring at the sunset. "You know the way?" he asked.

Ramona didn't answer.

"We can worry 'bout that in the morning," Ross said. "We need to get there first."

Carsten nodded in agreement.

***

As night fell, the fire blazed. Ross and the three gun hands sat in a circle, while Nash sat opposite them with his Bible.

"Hey, Carsten," Ike said as he cut a deck of cards, "you wanna join us for some poker?"

"Sure," Carsten said. "I ain't the best player, but there ain't much else to fill the time. You with us, Ramona?"

Ramona ignored the invitation, sharpening her bowie knife with a whetstone.

"I'll take that as a no," Carsten said as he sat with the others. "I figure Nash wouldn't be interested."

"It ain't Sunday," Ike said as he dealt the hands. "I don't fancy a sermon. Is he some kind of circuit preacher?"

"I'm stumped about him," Carsten replied as he looked at his cards. "He ain't a fan of cards or whiskey, and he spends most of his free time with his head buried in the Good Book. But I heard he's mighty dedicated to keepin' the peace. We'll see how he fares."

"I heard you got into some dangerous gunfights," Buford remarked.

"Well, it ain't somethin' worth braggin' about," Carsten said. He kept his focus on his cards rather than making eye contact with Buford.

"Guess he's a modest fella," Charlie said.

"Have you ever killed?" Carsten asked. "It ain't a feelin' that goes away like a hangover."

The others fell silent.

"My pa was a lawman," Carsten said. "He figured he could uphold things without takin' no lives. But he shot a man who was holdin' up a stagecoach and quit after that. Thought ranchin' would give him a less dangerous life. Then a year later, the brothers of the man he killed ended up tryin' to raid us."

"How old were you?" Buford asked.

"I was still between hay and grass," Carsten said.

"Are we gonna play cards or talk history?" Ike said, clearing his throat.

"I'd rather play cards," Carsten said, "if you don't mind. Past battles ain't a favorite conversational topic of mine."

"Agreed," Ross said. "We ought to get some sleep after this game. Let's say the winner takes the first watch."

***

After another day of riding, Carsten and the posse set up camp near Gold Canyon. He viewed the trail leading into the Hieroglyphic Mountains as he brushed down his horses.

"If Wiley Frye is anywhere, he's gonna be there," Ross said. "But he's likely to be waitin' to dry gulch anybody who gets too close. I want you and Ramona to scout things out in the morning."

"What do you reckon we'll find?" Carsten asked.

"There're caves and old mines in them mountain trails," Ross said. "I reckon Frye's holed up in any of those."

"He'll have an outpost set up closer to the trail," Ramona added. "But his men can come from anywhere."

"We'll keep this entrance covered in case anybody shows," Ross said.

"If there ain't another path there," Carsten said.

Chapter 7
Return of Old Enemies

Morris pulled his hat low as he glimpsed the morning sun while driving the herd to pasture on top of Blondie. His sweat-stained bandana did little to ease the dust kicked up by the steers or the smell of their flatulence. Attie rode ahead of the herd while Davey and Mike rode the flanks.

Upon reaching the pasture, Morris pulled the reins of his horse to stop him. As he watched the herd mill about, he noticed two riders on the trail riding toward the ranch. "Watch the herd," he said to the others. "I'm gonna see what business these fellas have 'round here." He turned his horse to face them and trotted forward.

"Howdy!" the first man said as they saw him approaching. They stopped their horses and turned toward him.

"What do you boys want?" Morris asked, easing the Henry rifle out of his saddle ring as he tried to recognize the man's voice. As they drew closer, he noticed they both had short haircuts on the verge of being bald. The first man wore a prospector's overalls, while the other wore some threadbare trail clothes.

"Is this the route to the McNeil ranch?" the second man said. "We're lookin' for Carsten McNeil."

"What's your business with him?" Morris asked.

"Does Carsten McNeil live here?" the first man asked.

"I'm askin' the questions," Morris growled, pointing the rifle at the pair. "And if'n I don't like your answers, I'd say you boys are trespassin'."

The two men raised their hands. "We got unfinished business with Carsten McNeil," the first man said.

Morris opened his mouth to reply when shots rang out behind him, followed by a thunder of hooves and frightened mooing. Morris snapped around to see the herd stampeding away as Mike and Davey spurred their horses after them.

"You yellow-bellied curs!" Attie screamed. She charged forward on Lancelot, firing her Peacemaker at the two riders.

"Attie!" he yelled, spurring his horse toward her.

There were more shots in the distance, as Davey and Mike fired their guns in the air to try to divert the stampeding cattle. The two riders rode in the opposite direction at full gallop. Attie rode after them. She continued firing at them, despite the hammer falling on empty chambers.

"Attie!" Morris yelled again. He lashed Blondie's reins and pursued her at a lope.

When Morris caught up with Attie further up the trail, she was cursing as Lancelot stood still. He returned the Henry rifle to the saddle ring and slowed Blondie to a walk as he drew closer. Attie tried to coax her horse further.

"Attie!" he yelled, grabbing her shoulder.

She turned to face him, her face contorted in rage. "Take your mitts off me!" she growled.

Morris removed his hand from her shoulder. "They've gone," he said. "And Lancelot's plain tuckered out. Let him rest." He extended his hand.

"Morris," Attie said as her voice cracked, "those were Big Al's boys. The ones who kidnapped me last year."

"That can't be," Morris replied. "Big Al's dead. And most of his associates are dead or in the hoosegow."

"I know what I saw," Attie said as tears welled in her eyes. "I'd recognize their faces anywhere."

"I believe you," Morris said as he hugged his sister. "Now let's go home. We'd best speak to Pa 'bout this. He and Ma will have probably heard the shootin' and be wonderin' what went down."

Attie nodded in agreement.

***

The midday sun began to heat the yard as Morris rode back into their yard. Attie was on Blondie's back, leading Lancelot behind them. He raised a hand as he approached the house. Vince hobbled out onto the porch, Cassie following behind, clutching the shotgun. Morris hitched Blondie by the corral, dismounting and helping his sister down.

"What's goin' on out there?" Vince asked. "We heard shootin'."

"Couple of uninvited guests," Morris said. "There was some shootin', and it caused a stampede. Davey and Mike are takin' care of the herd. I'm just bringin' Attie back here to calm down."

"What kind of uninvited guests?" Cassie asked as she took Attie's hand. "Were they rustlers?"

Morris shook his head.

"You'd best come inside and tell us what happened," Vince said.

Morris followed his sister and their parents inside, where they sat down at the kitchen table.

"We were puttin' the herd to pasture when two folks came down the trail," Morris said. "They was lookin' for Carsten."

"But Carsten lives in Prescott now," Cassie said.

"I know," Morris replied. "But I wasn't gonna share that with two strangers until I knew their intentions. They said they had unfinished business. It was round that time Attie recognized them and started shootin'."

Cassie gaped at Attie. "Who were they?" she asked her daughter.

"They were two of those men who kidnapped me last year," Attie replied. "I got scared and started shootin' 'fore they did anythin' else untoward."

"Are you sure?" Vince asked, leaning closer.

Attie nodded, and Vince turned to Morris.

"I ain't got no call not to believe her," Morris said. "They looked and sound familiar, and they said they had unfinished business with Carsten."

"But Big Al's cronies are dead or in jail," Vince said. "So what are they doin' here?"

"Whatever it is," Morris said, "it likely ain't good. They must have been sprung."

The door to the house swung open, prompting Morris to reach for his Peacemaker. As he saw Mike and Davey enter, he exhaled and loosed his grip on the gun.

"That Cavalry model ain't good for a quick draw," Vince said.

"Well, I always preferred range rather than speed," Morris replied. "How's the herd?"

"Tuckered out," Davey replied, as he sat down beside Attie. "Lost two of the smaller ones in the stampede, but that's about it."

"Thank the Lord," Cassie said.

"You boys used to tend to Big Al's ranch," Morris said. "You know the folks who kidnapped Attie?"

"Tucker and McElroy," Davey said, without hesitation. "We detained 'em for Carsten when we was deputy for Sheriff Horne. They ain't gun hands, but they used to perform the underhanded tasks for Big Al."

"But I thought they were both servin' time in Yuma," Vince said.

"Far as I know, they were." Davey said. "I remember one of them having messy blonde hair and the other had short white hair."

"The two folks I met on the trail had real short haircuts and could have been bald," Morris replied.

"Don't they give real short haircuts in jail?" Morris asked.

"I suppose," Vince said. "If that's the case, they likely escaped from the territorial prison."

"Then Carsten's in danger," Morris said, standing up. "I'd better ride into Cripple Gorge and warn Benny and Miss Fleur."

"I'll come with you," Attie said. "It'll be safer if we travel in pairs, like Carsten originally suggested."

"No," Vince said with a stern tone. "They might still be out there, and Lancelot needs rest. Mike can go with Morris. Attie, you need to learn to keep a level head. Your wild shooting could have killed someone you weren't planning on, either with the bullets or the stampede. Understood?"

"Yes, Pa," Attie said with a sigh.

"I'd best ride out," Morris said. "Should be back by dusk."

***

Sweat poured down Morris's face as he and Mike rode down the trail toward Cripple Gorge in the afternoon sun. They walked their horses up to the livery owned by Major Tobias Hughes. Morris noticed the major's son, Benedict Hughes, napping in the shade offered by the building, his hat pulled over his eyes.

"Hey, Benny!" Morris yelled, prodding Benny with his foot.

Benny grumbled as he stirred. "What is it?" he said as he lifted his hat. "Morris? What are you doin' here this time of day? Must be important if'n you're ridin' in the sun."

"It is," Morris said. "Can we talk to you someplace private?"

Benny scrambled to his feet. "C'mon in," he said. "I'm sure Pa won't mind."

"We need to head to Frenchie's," Morris said. "This concerns Miss Fleur too."

"Fine," Benny said, "but don't let it take too long."

"Do you mind if we stable our horses while we're here?"

"Help yourself," Benny said, pulling open the doors.

Mike stepped forward and pulled open the other door while Morris led the horses inside. After stabling the horses, Morris strolled up Cripple Gorge's main street with Benny and Mike. In the middle of the day, few people passed by. Morris stepped into the general store.

Frenchie slouched behind the counter, stirring as the shop bell rang. "Howdy, boys," he said. "What can I do you for?"

"We need to talk to Miss Fleur," Morris said. "It's real important, and her life could be in danger."

Frenchie stammered as he stood up.

Fleur entered the shop from the backroom.

"Ah, there you are, my dear," Frenchie said, trying to remain composed. "Mr. McNeil says he wants to talk to you."

"Mr. Carpentier," Morris said, "do you mind if we use your back room? We need to speak in private."

"Only if I can join you," Frenchie replied. "I'm not letting you get my daughter into trouble."

"Of course," Morris said. "This might concern you, too."

Frenchie held the door open to the back room and beckoned everyone inside. He then hung up a sign on the front door. As he followed Morris into the back room, he closed the door behind him.

"All right," he said. "What is the trouble?"

Morris took a deep breath. "Two of Big Al's men came by the ranch today," he said. "They were looking for Carsten. I reckon they sprang out of Yuma."

Fleur gasped. Frenchie crossed himself.

"You reckon they're gonna be comin' here?" Benny asked.

"I don't know," Morris said. "But I reckon you'd best be prepared."

"But Carsten don't live here no more," Benny said. "He lives in Prescott."

"I need to go to him," Fleur said. "I have to warn him."

"I forbid it," her father said, raising his voice. "They could be lyin' in wait."

"I agree," Morris said. "If they're on the run, they probably ain't gonna risk headin' into town. But they might try to dry gulch us on the trail. But they'll want to know where Carsten is, so I reckon they won't shoot us outright. What they'll do instead, that don't bear thinkin' 'bout."

"I could take the next stage to Prescott," Fleur said. "That way I'd be travelin' with others. And I'll be safe if I'm with Carsten. Besides, I can shoot. Y'all know that from when we rescued Attie from Big Al."

Morris exchanged a look with Mike, who shrugged. "Well, if your mind's made up," he said, "I ain't gonna get in your way."

"If you do this," Frenchie said, "You're going to be on your own. I can't leave the store unattended for too long."

"I got it," Fleur said. "And I won't be too long. I know Carsten's hotel, and I know Sheriff Horne is likely to be around."

Mike tapped Morris on the shoulder.

"We'd best be headin' back," Morris said, tipping his hat. "You folks take care now. And good look with your trip, Miss Fleur." He left the storeroom with Mike and Benny.

Chapter 8
Into the Mountains

A vicious prod woke Carsten the following morning. He saw Ramona standing over him and scrambled out of his bedroll.

"Chew some jerky and get saddled," Ramona said. "Vámanos!"

Carsten folded up his bedroll and carried it toward Bill.

"Leave the packhorse," Ramona said. "Take what you need, but we travel light. And try to keep up."

Carsten nodded in agreement, taking a box of cartridges from the saddlebags and placing it in his satchel. He saddled and mounted Dan, following Ramona as she rode toward the canyon. "Where are we headin'?" he asked as he brought his horse parallel to hers.

"There's a spring not far into the canyon," Ramona said. "I'd say that's the first place we check."

"Ain't gonna argue that," Carsten said.

Ramona halted and turned to face him. "From this point on," she said, pointing at him, "I don't want you makin' any more noise than you need to. No talkin', no yellin', and try to keep up. Hope your horse is surefooted and canny."

Carsten nodded in agreement. He flicked Dan's reins and followed her down the canyon trail.

***

Carsten's horse walked along the rocky terrain as he followed Ramona's lead. Five miles down the trail, Ramona gestured for him to halt. Carsten heard laughter in the distance as she dismounted and led her horse off the trail. Carsten followed as she gestured again. He hitched his horse to a bush and removed his Winchester from his saddle ring. She gestured for him to crouch while following her toward a cluster of rocks.

Taking up a position behind the rocks, Carsten noticed a campsite near a hot spring. Four men sat around a small cooking fire, drinking from a bottle of whiskey. As he surveyed the group further, he noticed another man lying hogtied near the horses.

"You reckon we should take 'em now?" Carsten whispered.

"Sí," Ramona said with a nod. "I recognize their captive. That's the Tombstone Kid. Some wannabe gunfighter, probably after the bounty."

"Then we're on the right trail," Carsten said. "And they don't seem like the attentive types. What do you reckon? Restrain them, then get the others?"

Ramona nodded.

"U.S. Marshals!" Carsten shouted from his position as he primed his Winchester. "Throw up your hands!"

He saw the men at the camp react. One of them reached for the six-shooter on his gun belt. Carsten fired a shot near his feet. The man dived for cover. Another shot rang out. Another man dropped back, clutching his abdomen.

"Anybody else with a problem?" Ramona asked. She emerged from behind the rocks and chambered the next round into her Winchester.

The other three men raised their hands. Carsten emerged and approached the campsite, keeping his rifle trained on the men.

"Oh, that's Ramona Vasquez!" the injured man yelled.

"That's a fact," Carsten said, "and you'd best do what she says. So unless you wanna end up like your friend there, you'd best ditch them gun belts."

He heard a clatter of metal and leather on stone as the men removed their gun belts and threw them at his feet.

"Now, get down on the ground," Carsten said. "Ramona, keep them covered while I get some cuffs on them."

"What about our friend?" one man said. "Ain't you gonna see to him?"

"The bounty's dead or alive, so I get paid either way," Ramona said. "If you value his life, you'll do as we tell you."

"She means it," Carsten added. "The sooner you get restrained, the sooner I can see to your partner there." Carsten handcuffed the three outlaws and directed them to sit by the cooking fire. He walked over to the man Ramona had shot and examined his wound. "How ya feelin' mister?" he asked.

"Cold," the outlaw replied. "Thirsty. Any chance of a drink?"

"It looks like I got him in the stomach," Ramona said. "He ain't gonna last the rest of the day."

Carsten bowed his head. He stood up and walked back toward the trail.

"Where are you goin'?" Ramona asked.

"Gettin' the horses," Carsten replied. "I left my canteen with Dan's saddle."

"Forget that," Ramona said. "You're soft, McNeil. Too soft for me to be workin' with you."

"Hey, I was hopin' to take 'em alive," Carsten said as he stopped and turned toward her.

"Good for you," Ramona said, rolling her eyes. "Then you can watch these three prisoners while I get the others. Good luck keepin' them in line. You'll be dead before I get back. Adiós." She shoved past Carsten as she strode away.

Carsten walked over to the outlaws' captive and cut him free.

"Much obliged, mister," he said, shaking Carsten's hand after spitting blood on the floor. The man looked no older than twenty and sported a black eye and swollen lips.

"You must be the Tombstone Kid," Carsten said. "And you're real lucky you're still breathin' right now. What you doin' out here?"

The Kid sat on a rock. "Heard there was a big bounty bein' offered by one railroad on some robbers," he said. "I thought I'd try to catch some."

"Since you ain't deputized," Carsten said as he looked back at the detained outlaws, "you ain't eligible for that reward. Now make yourself useful and help keep those men covered."

"You betcha," the Kid replied, picking up a discarded revolver and aiming it at the group. "I've killed five men and these rips ain't gonna be no trouble."

"Comin' from a fella who was trussed up like a hog less than five minutes ago," Carsten said with a grin. "I'm gonna take that with a mighty pinch of salt."

He sat down on a rock and kept his rifle trained on the outlaws. "Hey!" the Kid said with a forced scowl. "Are you callin' me a liar?"

"I never met a man who killed who bragged 'bout afterward as eager as you," Carsten said. "What was you doin' before you tried your hand at bounty huntin'?" From the corner of his eye, Carsten noticed the man fidgeting.

"I was a trail hand," the Kid said in a hushed tone.

"So was I," Carsten replied. "Ain't no shame in that."

"Hard work that pays pennies," the Kid said. "I wanted somethin' different. I wanted to be a gunfighter like the ones I'd read about in the dime novels."

"Stick to readin' 'bout them, Kid," Carsten said. "Now keep quiet so I can talk to the prisoners."

Carsten stood up and loomed over the three outlaws. He smelled coffee in a pot by the cooking fire.

"You folks mind if I have some of your coffee?" he asked.

"Help yourself," one outlaw replied. "It ain't like we're able to argue."

"Much obliged," Carsten said, tipping his hat. He picked up a tin cup and filled it from the pot. "Okay, we're gonna have a friendly chat. I'm lookin' for Wiley Frye. Any of you fellas seen him 'round here?"

One outlaw shrugged. Another shook his head.

"They're Frye's boys," the Kid said. "They mentioned him earlier when I got captured."

"Is that a fact?" Carsten asked the first outlaw. "In that case, you can help me with somethin' I've been ponderin'. Where is Mr. Frye right now, if he ain't at this camp? We expectin' him later? How many more men does he have? You share what you know, and I'll see the judge in Phoenix looks down kindly on you."

"That shavetail has a big imagination after readin' too many dime novels," the first outlaw said. "We don't ride with Wiley Frye. Wished we did, though. Always admired that fella's charisma."

"Frye's gonna be sendin' some of his boys down here," the injured man said through gritted teeth. "We sent someone to his main camp to ask 'bout the Kid there."

"Damn it, Jesse!" the first outlaw snapped. "You let the cat outta the bag!"

"Keep quiet!" the Kid said. He raised the revolver and cocked it.

Carsten felt his heart beating. He brandished his rifle as he heard rocks being disturbed. Instinct taking over, he dived to the ground as shots rang out.

A barrage of shots peppered the campsite. Carsten could feel the rock he'd sat on being chipped away as he lay prone behind it. He surveyed the brush and rock clusters for signs of gun smoke. From the corner of his eye, he noticed the Tombstone Kid lying face down on the ground. He heard crying emanating from behind the rocks where the outlaws had sat.

"Kid!" Carsten hissed. "Jesse."

"They both gone up the flume," one outlaw said. "And my friend's been hit."

"That's your reckonin', son," one of the other outlaws said with a cackle. "The señorita was right 'bout one thing: you'll be dead 'fore she gets back."

"I ain't a goner just yet," Carsten said, tightening his grip on his rifle.

He saw someone emerge from behind a rock cluster with a revolver in hand. Carsten peered down the sights of his Winchester. He fired. The man tumbled down. More shots. Carsten rolled from his position, glimpsing a muzzle flash behind some brush. He chambered the next round and fired. Another figure fell through the brush, clutching a rifle.

More shots rang out, this time behind Carsten. He spun around to see riders approaching. He smiled as he recognized Dan and Bill among the horses. The posse fired at the brush and the rocks surrounding the camp. Through the smoke, he noticed a third man tumble from his position. A fourth had stood up and fled in the opposite direction.

"After him!" Ross Cooper's voice echoed through the canyon.

Another gun cracked. The man dropped. Carsten took a deep breath, inhaling powder smoke. He stood up and nodded to the riders, seeing Nash holster his revolver.

"Carsten," Ross said as he approached. "You hurt?"

Carsten dusted himself off, noticing several bullet holes that passed through his coat. "Lord knows why, but I'm fine," he said. "This coat's gonna need some patches, though. Looks like I proved someone wrong." He grinned at Ramona.

"You were just lucky," she replied with a disdainful look. "Quaker McNeil, the leprechaun cowboy."

The other posse members laughed.

"I kinda like that," Carsten said. "It has a nice ring to it, but it's gonna be a mouthful."

"Any idea who those folks were?" Ross asked, indicating the three captives as the gun hands seated them back on the rock.

Carsten noticed blood seeping from a wound in one man's leg. "They definitely are Frye's boys," Carsten said. "The Tombstone Kid and the late Mr. Jesse sorta proved that." He walked over to the two bodies, closing Jesse's eyes. He stood back up and held his hat to his chest.

"Who's the kid?" Ross asked.

"Those boys had him as a captive," Carsten said as he kneeled by the Tombstone Kid's body. "Some poor kid who wanted to be a gunfighter after readin' those dime novels 'bout Wild Bill Hickok."

"In that case," Ross asked, "where's Frye himself?"

"You still got that handbill?" Carsten said as he looked around the camp.

"Sure." Ross produced the wanted poster and handed it over.

Carsten unfolded the handbill and looked over the other three bodies. As he closed their eyes, he compared their faces to the one on the poster. None of them matched. He turned to the marshal and shook his head.

"How are the captives?" Ross asked.

"One of them took a hit when the lead started flyin'," Carsten said as he walked back to where the prisoners were seated. "It seems them fellas were a little overzealous in their shootin' and took some of their own. Personally, I wouldn't want to be defendin' a partner who does a thing like that."

"So you reckon he's goin' to give up the rest of his flock?" Nash asked.

"That's my notion," Carsten said, kneeling beside the injured man. "We know you boys are ridin' with Wiley Frye, so there ain't no sense in denyin' it. Tell me what I want to know, and I'll see to it that leg of yours gets looked at by a doctor in Phoenix."

"Reckon I'm gonna lose it anyhow," the man said through gritted teeth. "It's a long ride back to Phoenix."

"Out of my way," Nash said while dismounting. "Let me put the fear of God in him." He shoved past Carsten and loomed over the captive.

"Hey!" Carsten said. "There ain't no call for that."

"Tell me what you know," Nash said to the captive, "or I'll give you a taste of what eternal damnation feels like."

"You pound sand, preacher man," the captive said.

Nash stomped on the man's wounded leg. He screamed. His two partners shuffled away as their faces turned pale.

"Tarnation!" the outlaw yelled.

"Shut up!" Nash shouted, stomping the wound again and prompting another scream.

"That's enough," Carsten said, positioning himself between Nash and the outlaw. "I ain't condonin' this."

"Your soft heart is admirable," Nash said, "but you shouldn't wear it for the souls of the damned." He grabbed Carsten and shoved him out of the way.

Carsten got back up and floored the deputy with a punch.

"Carsten!" Ross yelled.

Carsten saw Nash scrambling for the Colt Army in his holster. He drew his Remington and leveled it at him. "Your call, Deputy Nash," he said, thumbing back the hammer.

"That's enough!" Ross shouted, firing his gun into the air.

Nash moved his hand away from his revolver. Carsten uncocked his Remington and rotated the cylinder back to the empty chamber before holstering it.

"I will not have dissent among the ranks of my posse," Ross said. "Both of you will be on suspension when we return to Phoenix. If either of you have objections to that, you can leave right now."

"No, sir," Carsten said. He turned to the captive. "If you don't tell us what we want to know, I won't be able to protect you from Deputy Nash. Where is Wiley Frye hidin', and how many men does he have?"

"Okay," the prisoner spluttered. "There's a cave 'bout three miles east of here. That's where he makes camp. With the folks you killed here, he should have four other people with him."

"Much obliged," Carsten said.

"We can follow the trail left by the folks who jumped you," Ross said. "Charlie and Ike, you boys stay, load up these prisoners and bodies on the spare horses, and start headin' toward Phoenix 'fore the vultures get real nasty. Rest of you, with me."

Carsten mounted Dan. "You reckon he's heard the shootin'?" he asked Ross.

"I reckon," Ross said with a nod. "He'll be prepared for us, that's for sure."

Chapter 9
Fast Eddie

Tucker stared into the embers of the small fire. The horses stood nearby, silhouetted in the moonlight. He heard his stomach grumbling.

"We got any grub?" McElroy asked. "I'm hungrier than sin."

Tucker reached into his coat pocket and produced a small piece of jerky. "That's the last of it," he said as he tossed it over to his partner. "Reckon it'll only rouse your appetite without beddin' it down."

McElroy caught it and chewed it. "You think they're still chasin' us?" he asked as he lay back, resting his head on his saddle and looking toward the stars.

"That girl's horse was probably worn out a while back at the rate she rode after us," Tucker replied. "But I ain't riskin' goin' back to the ranch with a hurricane like that."

"For once, I agree with you," McElroy said. "So where do we go? They likely telegraphed someone in Cripple Gorge. Maybe even Prescott."

"Prescott," Tucker said. "I reckon we should head there."

"Are you crazy?" McElroy said. "That's the county seat. Everyone knows Sheriff Horne is tight with the McNeils."

"Well, the town's big enough to slip in unnoticed," Tucker replied. "Maybe we can ask around at the saloons. I'm sure there's gonna be some other folks with an ax to grind."

"Like who?" McElroy asked, not making eye contact.

"You remember Fast Eddie?" Tucker said.

"Yeah, I remember him," his partner said with a nod. "Used to brag 'bout the fastest gun in the territory since Johnny Ringo. Didn't he duel Carsten?"

"He did," Tucker said. "But Carsten shot his gun out of his hand. That's why they call him Quaker McNeil."

"So where do we find him?" McElroy asked as he sat up.

"Hell if I know," Tucker replied. "If he ain't in the hoosegow or the bone orchard, he's gonna be driftin'."

"You reckon he'll be in Prescott too?" McElroy said. "Bet he'll be wantin' a rematch with Carsten."

"That's what I was figurin' too," Tucker said. "Now I'm gonna get some sleep 'fore we sneak into town."

***

The sun was rising as Tucker and McElroy rode into Prescott. Few people wandered the streets, save for the occasional shopkeeper opening up a storefront. Tucker followed the signs to Whiskey Row. Shops gave way to saloons, bordellos, and gambling halls. Tucker pointed to one saloon ahead, signposted as the Lame Horse.

The saloonkeeper emerged from the batwing doors, carrying another man by the lapels. "Get outta here, ya drunk!" he said. "And don't let me catch you in here again, or else I'm callin' the sheriff!" He threw the man from the porch, sending him sprawling into the front street.

"You'll pay for that, mister!" the former patron slurred. "I'm the fastest gun in the territory since Johnny Ringo, and I'm callin' you out!"

"Not without this, you ain't," the bartender said, holding up a gun belt with a Schofield in its holster.

Tucker looked at the patron. He wore a wide-brimmed hat swept up at the front and a red silk bandana, both of which looked threadbare. A five-o'clock shadow adorned his face. "That must be him," he said to McElroy.

The bartender looked up to see Tucker staring. "What are you fellas lookin' at?" he said. "We're closed. This don't concern you."

"We got business with your friend there," Tucker said. He dismounted and walked toward the pair.

"Yeah," the patron said, "you're in for it now."

"Take him and go before I get the sheriff," the bartender said. "You ain't welcome in my establishment."

"Jonesy," Tucker said as he pulled the patron's arm over his shoulders. "Keep hold of the horse, will ya?"

"Whatever you say, Smithy," McElroy said as he dismounted and led the two horses.

"Can you give this fella back his shootin' iron?" Tucker asked the bartender.

"Not until he's sobered up," the bartender said.

"That's my gun, you thievin' polecat!" the patron said. "I'll get you for this."

"Come on, Eddie," Tucker said. "Let's get outta here before we draw more attention to ourselves." He led Eddie away as McElroy followed with the horses.

As they walked away from the saloon, Tucker made a cursory glance behind him. The bartender walked back into his establishment.

"Are you folks joinin' me for a drink?" Eddie said. "Forget it. I don't drink with folks like you."

"If'n we're drinkin' anythin'," Tucker replied, "it's gotta be coffee. We need to talk to you, Eddie."

"How do you know my name's Eddie?" he said. "Are you comin' to prove your mettle?"

Tucker recoiled at the smell of whiskey on Eddie's breath as the drunk gunslinger laughed. "We came to ask for your help. It's regardin' a fella named Carsten McNeil."

"I know that fella," Eddie said, wrenching himself from Tucker's grasp. "Let me at him. He's a dead man walkin'." He stepped forward and fell to the ground.

Tucker prodded him with his foot. He snored. "Jonesy, find a place to hitch them horses so we can sober this fella up."

"Right," McElroy said. "You sure this is the fella we want?"

"No," Tucker replied. "But he's a seasoned gun hand, or at least he was. And he's probably got a vengeful streak wider than the Colorado River directed toward our mutual friend." He noticed a horse trough in front of another saloon across the street, the Silver Dollar. He nodded to McElroy.

His partner led their horses to a hitching post before returning to help carry Eddie and dunk him in the trough. The gunfighter spat out water, coughing and spluttering.

"You awake, mister?" Tucker asked.

Eddie said something incoherent and went back to sleep. Tucker dunked him in the trough again.

The saloon doors opened behind them. "Can I help you fellas?" a woman's voice said.

Tucker pulled Eddie out of the trough as he watched a large woman in a plain dress approach. "Tryin' to sober this fella up," he replied. "You got coffee?"

"Well, we just opened for breakfast," she said. "Bring him inside."

"Much obliged," McElroy said, tipping his hat.

***

The smell of fresh coffee combined with the biscuits and gravy the cook served up made Tucker's mouth water.

"I've missed breakfasts like this," McElroy said between mouthfuls. "Makes a real change from that gruel they served up in Yuma."

Eddie groaned as he massaged his temples.

"This'll help that," Tucker said, pointing to Eddie's plate.

Eddie gave a thankful nod as he tucked into the biscuits and gravy on the plate. "Remind me again," Eddie said after taking a long gulp of coffee, "who are you folks and what do you want with me? You ain't lawmen, that's for sure."

Tucker looked around. Other than a bartender, nobody else occupied the saloon. "You remember Alphonse Moraday?" he asked Eddie in a hushed tone.

Eddie shrugged.

"Big fella," McElroy said. "Wanted to buy up the county. He always traveled with some John Bull."

"English Bill?" Eddie asked. "I remember him. I heard someone finally killed him."

"Well," Tucker said, "we used to be on Moraday's payroll, same as you. But we crossed paths with a fella named Carsten McNeil. And that's the same someone who killed English Bill."

Eddie set down his cutlery and glared at Tucker. For a second, he looked sober. "I got a major ax to grind with Carsten McNeil," he said. "That kid beat me in a draw and let me live. Now everyone's forgotten who I am. They just laugh me off." He raised his right hand, showing the scar from where Carsten's shot had made its mark a year ago.

"My heart bleeds for you," Tucker said. "But we got a plan in mind. We're lookin' for Carsten. I heard he's a deputy marshal in these parts."

"He ain't in Prescott," Eddie said, nursing his coffee cup. "I've been lookin' for him, too."

"If'n you stick with us," Tucker said, "we might find him."

"How?" Eddie said. "I been in Prescott for the past couple days, and I ain't seen him. And I ain't settin' foot in Cripple Gorge again. His family has a farm in this county, right?"

Tucker exchanged a nervous glance with McElroy, who looked down at the table. "We've… been there," he said. "Carsten ain't there. And they're likely gonna shoot us on sight if we pay 'em another visit."

"Why don't we take a walk?" Eddie said. "I gotta get my gun back from the other place."

***

The streets had gotten busier by the time Tucker and his companions left the saloon. He saw carriages and wagons rolling past at the end of the street, while the occasional rider trotted down Whiskey Row. As they reached the Lame

Horse, Eddie pushed past Tucker and strode through the doors. Tucker followed close behind.

Like the Silver Dollar, the Lame Horse was empty except for the saloonkeeper and three older patrons around one table. They stopped playing their poked game and stared at Eddie and Tucker as they entered.

"You again?" the saloonkeeper growled. "I thought I told you to skedaddle."

"You did," Eddie replied, sounding more composed than he had. "But you've got something of mine, and I'd very much like it back."

Tucker stepped toward the bar. "Just give 'im the gun, son," he said. "It'll be a lot easier on everybody if you do." He heard a scrape of chairs. He turned and saw the three patrons standing up.

"You ain't got no right to come in here and threaten Chester," one of the poker players said.

The sound of a hammer clicking made the men pause. McElroy aimed his revolver at them.

"You old-timers had best back down," Tucker said. "We ain't here to cause no trouble, but I ain't in the mood to be dealin' with folks who wanna give me trouble."

"Fine," Chester said, slamming his fist on the bar. "Take your gun and get the hell out of here." He produced Eddie's gun belt from behind the bar and threw it to him.

"That takes care of one thing," Eddie said as he fastened the belt, "but I still got business here. You owe me a showdown, mister."

"We ain't her for that," Tucker said, grabbing Eddie's arm. "We got what we came for. Now let's get outta here." He looked at Chester, who looked at him with wide eyes. "You have a good day now," he said to the petrified bartender, tipping his hat to the three patrons as he pulled Eddie out of the saloon.

***

"You want to recruit me, but you don't want to fight?" Eddie asked, scowling at Tucker as they walked down Whiskey Row.

"We're outlaws," Tucker said in a low voice. "We're takin' a big enough risk bein' here, as is. Don't want to get into no gunfight. We don't need to and draw attention."

Eddie's eyes narrowed as he stared at Tucker, but his stare softened as he relented. "Well, Carsten ain't here like I said. So where do we go?"

"That's what we figured on askin' you," McElroy said. "We ain't goin' back to the ranch, and Cripple Gorge is too small to get 'round unnoticed."

"Hold that thought," Eddie said, raising his hand to hush the pair.

Tucker followed Eddie's gaze to a stagecoach coming to a halt at the end of the street. He saw a young raven-haired woman in her early twenties exiting the stagecoach.

"Back!" Eddie hissed, ducking into a nearby alleyway.

Tucker followed him. Eddie peered out of the alleyway. His gaze remained affixed to the girl.

"What's the deal?" Tucker whispered.

"That girl there," Eddie said as he pointed at her. "I've seen her before. In Cripple Gorge. She was there when I confronted the McNeil boy and his old man. I saw the way they both looked at each other."

"So what's she doin' here?" McElroy asked.

"That's what we're gonna find out," Eddie said with a grin. "We're gonna follow her, and she's gonna lead us straight to Carsten."

Tucker nodded, rubbing his hands.

Chapter 10
Wiley Frye

Carsten said nothing as Dan trotted along toward the cave. The rockier terrain and lack of an obvious trail slowed their pace, and he felt his horse bob and weave as he found a path. He looked ahead at Nash, scowling at the deputy as he rode past.

Buford said, "I'm thinkin' we ought to have more horses to take back those boys near the spring. They're gonna get real ripe in this heat."

"I reckon so," Carsten said, not making eye contact.

"It's gonna be one hell of a time getting folks back to the trail from the cave," Buford said.

"I reckon so," Carsten said again.

"Don't feel bad 'bout layin' that preacher out," Buford said. "I would have done the same. His attitudes don't sit well. Refuse whiskey and cards, sure. I ain't gonna fault a fella for wantin' that. But enforce that will on everyone else, and we got a problem."

"It ain't his hate of cards and whiskey that's eatin' me," Carsten said. "It's how he treats folks who have surrendered. Wanted criminal or not, nobody deserves to be treated that way. Start gettin' brutal like that and you're no better than the folks you're huntin'."

Ramona suppressed a chuckle at his remark. "How long you been a lawman for, Quaker?" she asked.

"If it's any of your business," he replied, "just over a year."

"And still with that naivete," Ramona said, "It's a miracle you're still breathin'. You really are a leprechaun cowboy. Your family's Irish, right?"

"Scottish, far as I know," Carsten said. "But don't expect me to wear a kilt or play bagpipes."

"All right, keep it quiet," Ross said. "We don't want sound carryin' more than it already has."

***

The late afternoon sun bore down on the posse as a large cave came into view.

"We'd best dismount," Ross said. "We're sittin' ducks if we ride in shootin'."

Carsten nodded in agreement. He hitched his horse near a rock and removed his Winchester from the saddle ring. He crouched down as he followed Ross up a narrow trail. As they reached the cave mouth, Ross gestured for the posse to halt. Carsten tightened his grip on the rifle as Ramona crept into the cave. She turned to him and Ross, pointing inside and raising four fingers and her thumb.

"Five of them inside," Ross mouthed as he looked at Carsten. "Just play along and let me do the talkin'."

Carsten watched Ramona creep back out. She picked up a rock and threw it inside. Shots echoed within the cave. Carsten pressed against the rocks.

"Who's out there?" someone inside called out.

"U.S. Marshals!" Ross shouted back. "We got you trapped, Frye, so you might as well come out with your hands up!"

"How many of you out there?" the voice called.

"I got ten men and ten rifles out here pointin' in there!" Ross yelled. "Plus another fella settin' up dynamite. If you don't surrender in five minutes, he's gonna blast the cave entrance shut and leave y'all to rot."

A chuckle emanated from within the cave. "You ain't got ten guns out there," Wiley called out. "There's five of you. I been keepin' eyes on y'all ever since you rode into the mountains. I guess God ain't the only fella who's all-seein'."

"You'll face damnation for saying things like that!" Nash shouted, causing Carsten to roll his eyes.

"I'll face damnation for a lot of things, padre," Wiley replied with a confident tone. "What difference does one blasphemous boast make? What you doing out here anyhow? Was preachin' fire and brimstone to your flock not satisfyin' enough?"

"If you've been watchin' us," Ross said, "then you know we apprehended three of your men by the spring and killed five more."

Carsten felt his heart beating as he listened to the conversation.

"I know," Wiley said. "And those boys got a little too trigger-happy for my tastes, but they was all desperate men. Blow that dynamite 'cause I ain't goin' nowhere."

Carsten exchanged a glance with Ross as he heard whistling from within the cave. As he listened, he recognized the tune as "A-Hunting We Will Go." He looked back at

Buford, who exchanged a shrug. "What do we do?" Carsten whispered. "He's seen through our bluff."

"Stay put," Ross said. "We need to try to draw him out."

Carsten looked around. "I'm gonna see if I can get closer," he whispered. "Keep them busy while I move to where Ramona is." He crawled into the cave, grimacing as he pressed against the rocks.

"Well," Ross called, "you figured we can't seal you in here, but we can still starve you out."

"Oh, I've been ready for someone to come and stamp me out for some time," Wiley said. "I got plenty of food and water in this here cave. And there's a lot more to go around, thanks to you and your deputies."

Carsten grimaced at the remark as he arrived at Ramona's position. He surveyed the area, seeing five men positioned behind a barricade of crates around the corner from the cave entrance. Looking around, he noticed a string of horses tethered nearby. He tapped Ramona on the shoulder and pointed to the horses. She gave an approving nod as he shuffled toward them.

"Hey!" one of Wiley's men shouted.

A gunshot. Carsten felt a stone fragment hit the back of his neck. He returned fire. More shots echoed. He pressed against the ground, digging himself into a small depression on the cavern floor. He looked back toward the cave entrance. Ross, Nash, and Buford moved in. Carsten peered upward. Wiley's gang focused their fire on him. He took a shot at an exposed limb through the smoke.

Two men emerged from the back of the cave toward the horses. The echoing gunfire drowned out their frightened whinnying. Carsten fired a shot at the two men. One fell. The other dived behind the horses. Carsten laid down the rifle and drew his Colt Frontier. He fired two shots toward the horses and sprang out of cover, running toward an unguarded portion of the barricade. He vaulted over.

Through the smoke, Carsten glimpsed the bodies of Wiley's men. He saw Wiley Frye, recognizing the diagonal scar that ran across his face. The outlaw crouched behind the crates, breaking open a sawn-off shotgun.

As he ejected the shells, Carsten drew and cocked his Remington. "Hold it! Cease fire!"

Wiley looked up as the shooting stopped. "I know you," the outlaw said with a grin. "You're Quaker McNeil. You did this territory a favor by killin' off that Big Al last year. So why you stompin' me out too?"

"Drop that gun," Carsten said. "If you've heard of me, you know I'm fast on the draw."

"I don't doubt it," Wiley said as he complied. "And I ain't gonna ask you to prove it."

"Wise move," Carsten said.

"Have you got him?" Ross called.

"Yeah," Carsten replied as he removed a revolver and a bowie knife from Wiley's belt. "I got him."

"Then you'd best take me back," Wiley said.

Ross approached Carsten and Wiley, flanked by Ramona and Nash. "You hit?" he asked.

"I'm fine," Carsten replied, shaking his head. "Anyone else?"

"We're all good," Ross said as he cuffed Wiley's hands behind his back. "Wiley Frye, you're under arrest for the Desert Flyer robbery."

Wiley burst out laughing. "Are you kidding?" he said. "I would have loved the haul from that."

"Well, you seem supplied well," Buford remarked as he picked around. "Must've spent it quickly."

"It ain't the marshals I'm hidin' from," Wiley said.

"Then who?" Carsten asked.

After a moment of hesitation, Wiley said, "El Presidente."

"Carsten!" Ross snapped. "Get this fella on one of them horses. We're leavin'. Gag him if ya have to. Heard this fella can talk his way out of anything."

"Come on," Carsten said, gesturing with his Remington. "Buford, get over here! Help me tie him to the horse."

***

The late afternoon sun greeted the posse as they left the cave. Carsten returned to Dan while leading one horse out. Wiley sat in the saddle, his hands still cuffed behind his back and his legs tethered together beneath the horse's body. Carsten watched as Nash and Ramona led the other horses outside, using them to carry the bodies of Wiley's gang.

Carsten mounted Dan and watched as Ross led the posse along, riding at a trot. He looked at Buford, who mounted his own horse and led Wiley's mount along. Carsten clicked his tongue to prompt Dan to move. He noticed a small trail leading from the cave.

"You can't take me back to Phoenix," Wiley said as they rode along the trail. "If you found me, then el Presidente will have found me, too."

"Who is this Presidente fella?" Carsten asked.

"He's the one who orchestrates all the heists in this here territory," Wiley replied. "No bank, stagecoach, or train out here gets robbed without el Presidente knowin' 'bout it. And he always gets his cut."

"This man is spinning falsehoods," Nash said. "He is the serpent of Eden."

"So's the bartender in Phoenix, or the faro dealer in Tombstone," Buford said with a chuckle.

"Quite right," Carsten said. "Just tell me who this Presidente fella is, and I'll bring him to justice. I'll even put in a good word with the judge 'bout you."

"Thanks, that's real helpful," Wiley said. "But I can't tell you who he is."

"Come on," Carsten said. "You said he's gonna kill you. Might as well share what you know 'fore he does. I figure that'll take priority over whatever passes for honor among thieves."

"I can't describe a fella I never met," Wiley said.

Carsten said nothing. He shook his head as he contemplated the remark.

As the trail led from the foothills into open prairie, Carsten brought his horse parallel to Ross's mount. He noticed the peak of Turk's Head appearing before him. "What do you make of Wiley's story, sir?" he asked.

"Sounds a little too tall for me," Ross said. "If there was a Presidente, we'd know 'bout him. But if he's never seen the fella and there ain't no warrants outstandin', it's gonna sound like some wild goose chase."

Carsten nodded in agreement.

Wiley cackled behind them. "I knew you wouldn't believe me," he said. "But you wait and see, and you'll be sorry."

"I'll bear that in mind," Ross said, raising his hand for quiet. "Buford, can you do us a favor?"

"Sure thing, Marshal," Buford replied.

Carsten turned around to see Buford fasten a length of cloth in Wiley's mouth, muffling the outlaw's laughs. "What's up?" Carsten said, following Ross's gaze toward the mountain.

"Thought I seen somethin' up on Turk's Head," the marshal replied. "Somethin' ain't right."

A shot echoed from the mountain like thunder. The horses whinnied. Buford fell from his saddle. Wiley's horse bolted toward him and Ross.

"Find cover!" Ross yelled, pointing toward a large clump of brush.

Ramona and Nash let go of the horses with the bodies, spurring their horses toward the brush. Carsten rode back toward Wiley. He leaped from his saddle onto Wiley's horse as another shot rang out. The two men tumbled toward the ground, along with Wiley's horse.

Carsten winced as he looked up. He heard Wiley groaning and saw him pinned beneath his motionless horse, his gag shaken loose. "Are you hit?" he asked the captive.

"Cut my leg free before he shoots again!" Wiley hissed.

Carsten drew his knife and cut the cord binding Wiley's legs, allowing him to move it behind the carcass. He stared at the mountain, glimpsing signs of smoke. He looked toward the trail, seeing the rest of the posse had reached the brush and lay prone.

"Carsten?" Ross called.

"I'm here!" he replied. "Wiley's horse is down, and his leg's pinned under it, but he's alive!"

"Stay where you are!" Ross said. "They could jump us at any minute!"

Carsten pressed to the ground as much as he could, trying to stay behind the dead horse. "It'll be better for you if you call off your boys," he said to Wiley.

"They ain't my boys," Wiley replied. "You and your partners there wiped my boys out."

Carsten opened his mouth to speak and then paused as he contemplated his words. He looked around and saw Dan wandering on the trail. He whistled. Dan stopped in his tracks. Carsten noticed his Winchester in the saddle ring. His fist tightened. "All right," he said to Wiley in a low tone. "What do you reckon is gonna happen?"

"If there's more of 'em," Wiley said, "they'd be layin' down fire. But there's only been a couple of shots. I reckon there's just one fella on that cliff."

"Throw out your hat," Carsten said as he surveyed the side of the cliff. "Since I'm stumped, I might as well try to prove what you're sayin'."

"You gotta take these cuffs off me first," Wiley replied.

"That ain't a good idea," Carsten said.

"No, it ain't," Wiley said. "But what choice you got, lawman? I'm unarmed, my leg's pinned, and if I stick my head above my dead horse, it's gonna get blown clean off. So take off my damn cuffs!"

Carsten pulled a spare handcuff key from his pocket and unlocked Wiley's handcuffs.

"Much obliged," Wiley said, rubbing his wrists and removing his hat. "Just give the word."

Carsten drew his Colt Frontier and surveyed the cliff-side. He knew he was too far away to hit the attacker with his pistol, and he didn't want to expose himself to them by making a grab for the rifle on his horse.

"Now!" he hissed. From the corner of his eye, he saw Wiley's hand move. Another shot. Carsten glimpsed a muzzle flash on the side of the cliff. He fired a shot at them.

"Carsten?" Ross yelled, "what are you doin'?"

"Shoot where I'm shootin'!" Carsten replied, firing another round at the spot where he'd seen the muzzle flash.

A cacophony of gunfire sounded from the brush. Carsten took a deep breath. He jumped out from behind the horse and ran toward Dan. He leaped toward the saddle, getting his foot into one stirrup while trying to stay behind the horse as much as he could.

"Come on, Dan," he mumbled as the horse galloped toward the cliff. "If this sniper's any good, he'll be aimin' at me rather than you."

As he reached the cliff, Carsten dropped from his horse. The shooting from the brush died down. He pressed against the rock and shuffled along, looking up to see any sign of movement from the cliff.

The sound of a horse's breathing caught Carsten's attention, then he noticed a trail leading to the top of the cliff. A hobbled horse sat near the trail. Carsten grinned. The hunter would become the hunted, he thought.

Above him, he heard hurried footsteps on loose stone. Somebody running down the hill. He drew his Remington and crouched down. The sound of running passed by him. He noticed a man with a gray kepi and a Sharps rifle dashing toward the hobbled horse. He ducked back as the man looked behind him. Peering toward the trail, he noticed the man stow the rifle in a saddle ring and loosen the rope he used to hobble his mount.

Carsten emerged and cocked the Remington. "Put your hands up and turn around slowly," he said. "U.S. Marshal."

The man stopped.

"For an outlaw springin' another outlaw," Carsten added, "you sure like to shoot real close."

The man turned around, and Carsten noticed the revolver on his belt. "Wiley ain't a partner," he said. "He's a traitor."

He kicked dust in Carsten's face. Carsten shielded his eyes. He heard a click. He fired. The horse whinnied, followed by labored breathing. Carsten's eyes watered, blurring his vision. As it cleared, he saw the man on the ground, clutching a bleeding stomach wound with his left hand while gripping his revolver in his right.

"You… murderer…" he said, struggling to raise his gun.

Carsten walked over and grabbed his arm, wrenching the pistol out of his grip and uncocking it. "So who does Wiley ride with?" he asked. "Who did he betray?"

The sniper laughed and exhaled. A silence followed.

Carsten stood up and kicked dust over him.

"Carsten?" Ross called in the distance.

Carsten turned around to see him trotting toward his position, keeping his Winchester poised.

"Right here!" Carsten replied. "I got the sharpshooter. Looks like he was workin' alone."

"Is he still breathin'?" Ross asked.

"No, he's a goner," Carsten said, removing his hat and holding it to his chest.

Ross approached the hobbled horse and looked at the body.

"I know that fella," he said. "That's Corporal Jack Dixon, or Dixie Jack, as some folks call him. Former Confederate sharpshooter. You're lucky to have closed the distance without pickin' up a new hole in your head."

"Well, I figured he wasn't gonna shoot my horse," Carsten replied. "That'd have given me somethin' to hide behind. He seems fond of them gray threads. But the Civil War's been over for some time now. Was he some Lost Causer or somethin'?"

"Somethin' like that," Ross said, lighting a stogie. "Liked to present himself as such, but he was just a gun for hire."

"Well, he definitely seemed to be gunnin' for Wiley," Carsten said as Dan trotted up to him. "Said he was a traitor."

"A traitor?" Ross said with a sneer. "Wiley Frye's always been a man to lead rather than follow. I can't think of anybody he'd ride with."

"Well, we can't ask Dixie there," Carsten said as he mounted his horse.

"Nope," Ross said. "C'mon, let's get back to the posse. Buford's dead, if you're wonderin'."

Carsten nodded. As he followed the marshal, he contemplated Wiley's and Dixie's words. "Marshal," he said, "I don't know 'bout you, but I reckon we ought to find out more about this Presidente fella."

Chapter 11
A Surprise Reunion

A day later, the posse arrived back at Phoenix. Carsten felt a crowd staring as they rode through the streets with Wiley Frye and the pack horses loaded with corpses. He held his breath as the hot weather accentuated the smell of rot.

Sheriff Garrett loitered outside the marshal's office. He gave a slow clap as the posse rode in. "Well done, Marshal Cooper," he said. "Nice work on catchin' the elusive Wiley Frye. I've been after that fella for years."

"Pity I ain't wanted for nothin' in Maricopa," Wiley said as Nash pulled him off Buford's horse.

"Keep quiet," the deputy marshal hissed to him.

"Or what?" Wiley replied. "You'll ask Satan for a sharper pitchfork?"

Nash shoved Wiley to the ground.

"That's enough!" Ross shouted.

Carsten dismounted and helped Wiley to his feet, leading him into the marshal's office.

"Carsten," Garrett said with a false sincerity, "it's nice to see you made it back, okay."

Carsten ignored him.

Another deputy sat in the sheriff's office and nodded to Carsten as he led Wiley to the cell. "You look like you've been to hell and back," he commented.

"That ain't too far from the truth," Carsten said as he opened the cell door. He removed Wiley's handcuffs and beckoned him into the cell.

"You're a polite one, I'll give you that," Wiley said as he stepped inside. "Better than the preacher out there."

"I'll make sure Nash doesn't guard you," Carsten said as he locked the door. "He's a little too hard on people for my likin', no matter what side of the law they seem to be on."

"Amen to that," Wiley said as he lay on the cot in the cell.

"Listen," Carsten said, "you mentioned somethin' 'bout el Presidente. Now you're outta danger. You think you'd be willin' to share more 'bout who that big bug is?"

"Just 'cause I'm behind bars don't mean I'm outta danger," Wiley said while staring at the ceiling. "You can forget it, lawman. I ain't sayin' nothin' if I don't see no profit in it for me."

"I sure hope you can sleep on that thought," Carsten said. "You know, that sniper was a gun for hire called Dixie Jack. He said you were a traitor but didn't say who you betrayed. Was it el Presidente?"

Wiley turned away from Carsten and began to snore.

"Think about talkin'," Carsten added. "The trip back has led me to believe there's some truth in what you said, but I doubt the judge will share that belief." Carsten bowed his head as he left the office.

An undertaker was measuring the bodies lashed to the horses when he got outside. Ross stood and watched them while counting out a wad of bills.

"Has Mr. Alden paid out?" he asked the marshal.

"Yup," Ross said, pulling some bills aside. "Here's your cut. All told, it came to 'bout a hundred fifty each. Buford has a sister in Tucson, so I've arranged for his share to be wired to her."

"Much obliged," Carsten said as he counted the money.

"Come on," Ross said as he gave Carsten a friendly thump on the back. "Let's get a drink and celebrate. I'm buyin' the first round."

Carsten gave a small smile and nodded in agreement. A few passers-by tipped their hats as Carsten and Ross walked down the street.

"Sir," Carsten said, "I gotta voice some worries I have 'bout Deputy Pete Nash, regardin' his treatment of folk in custody."

"I know you do," Ross said. "Nash is dedicated to enforcin' the law, believin' it's next to godliness. But one of these days, he's gonna cross the wrong fella and get himself killed. However, I can't have you layin' him out like you did on the trail. It reflects badly on the U.S. Marshals Service, havin' dissent like that."

Carsten said nothing as he listened to Ross's lecture.

"Hey," the marshal said, "you listenin' to me?"

"Yes, sir," Carsten replied. "Just thinkin' 'bout what you're sayin'."

"Don't worry 'bout it," Ross said. "You did a great service today, apprehending Wiley Frye and killin' Dixie Jack. You deserve a little loafin' time."

"Sure," Carsten said. "I could use a splash of whiskey to unwind."

"Somethin' else is eatin' you," Ross stated.

"Yup," Carsten replied.

"That Presidente fella," Ross said. "He's probably some ghost story, Carsten. Don't let it worry you. The judge ain't gonna believe it anyhow."

"Not gonna believe what?" Sheriff Garrett said as he appeared behind them. "If you gentlemen are headin' for the Old Hunter Saloon, I'd be happy to buy a round for your posse from the county budget."

"That'll look funny at the bank," Ross said. "You didn't lift a finger to help go after Frye. Now you want to celebrate us bringin' him in."

"I already told you," Garrett replied, "he'd gone to ground in Pinal County. Last time I checked, I was the sheriff of Maricopa County. It was outta my hands. But enough about jurisdictional dilemmas. Who ain't gonna believe what? That sounds like a good story."

"Just some tall yarn that got cooked up on the trail," Carsten said. "Some mythical legendary outlaw called el Presidente. Apparently Wiley reckons this fella's gunnin' for him, after we got bushwhacked on the trail by Dixie Jack." He stared at the sheriff, noticing him twitch for a moment before chuckling.

"Well, he sounds like some larger-than-life dime-novel villain," Garrett said with a grin.

"He do, don't he?" Carsten said, laughing again. "Well, we'd best get them whiskeys in."

"That sounds like a plan," Garrett said.

Carsten laughed with Garrett.

"Carsten!" Fleur's voice echoed from across the street as they walked past the station.

"Fleur?" Carsten said to himself. He noticed Fleur waving to him from outside the station.

"Who's Fleur?" Garrett asked.

"My sweetheart," Carsten replied. "Will you excuse me? I might have to take a rain check on that drink." Carsten stepped away from Ross and Garrett. He crossed the street to the station and embraced Fleur. "What's goin' on?" he asked. "Did you get my letter?"

"No," she said, looking up at him. "I didn't get any letters. Sheriff Horne told me you'd gone to Phoenix."

"Well, I'm glad you're here," Carsten replied, beaming with a radiant grin. "Are you hungry? We could find somewhere to eat."

"Carsten," she said, "I came here to warn you about something. Two of Alphonse Moraday's men have escaped from prison and made their way to Cripple Gorge. Attie recognized them when they visited the ranch."

"Oh Lord," Carsten said, holding her close. "Don't worry. I'm comin' back soon. My work here's done anyhow." He leaned in to kiss her.

"Well, ain't that a touching reunion?" a familiar voice said nearby, punctuated by the sound of two guns cocking.

Carsten heard his own heart beating. He looked up. Three rough-looking men left the station and approached him. Two of them had revolvers drawn and pointed at him and Fleur. His eyes widened as he recognized the third man's wide-brimmed hat and red bandana.

Several people walked away from the area at a brisk pace. Others ran into the nearby houses or storefronts, closing doors and shuttering windows.

"Fast Eddie…" Carsten said, directing Fleur to stand behind him. "I'm surprised to see you're still breathin'. And I'm guessin' your buddies there are Byron Tucker and Glen McElroy, who should be servin' their sentences in Yuma Territorial Prison."

"I'll be breathin' a lot better once you pay me what you owe," he said, limbering his fingers. "Carsten McNeil…"

"Eddie," Carsten said as he held his hands out, "Big Al's dead. You ain't gotta worry 'bout your contract with him no more. He ain't gonna pay you from perdition."

"It ain't about the money," Eddie replied. "I was Fast Eddie, the quickest draw in the territory since Johnny Ringo. Until Quaker McNeil beat me. Now I'm a joke. I have to do this for my reputation."

"You don't gotta do this," Carsten stated with a confident tone. "Nobody's the fastest gun forever. You're lucky you made it out of our last gunfight still breathin'. Don't push that luck." He exchanged glances with Tucker and McElroy, noting the guns they had trained on him.

"I figured you'd be wantin' to talk me into backin' down," Eddie said with a sneer, "which is why I partnered up with these boys. We followed your sweetheart in the hopes she'd lead them to you. Now I'm callin' you out and givin' you a choice. Face me, or my boys will gun you and the pretty Miss Fleur down right where you stand."

"No!" Fleur yelled.

"It's all right," Carsten whispered to her. "They're a mite jumpy, so we ain't got much choice right now."

"What's it gonna be?" Eddie said. "I'm waitin' for an answer."

"When and where?" Carsten asked, patting his holster.

"Right here, right now," Eddie said. He gestured to Tucker and McElroy.

They advanced on the couple and grabbed Fleur.

"Hey!" she yelled as they pulled her away from Carsten.

McElroy aimed his revolver at Carsten and shook his head, wagging his finger. Tucker wrapped his arm around Fleur's neck, pointing his revolver at her head.

"Let her go, you rowdy-dow rip!" Carsten said. "If'n you want your showdown, let her go right now."

Eddie said, tutting, "That ain't like the gallant cowboy I took you for. But you ain't in a position to be makin' demands on me. You'd best take your position. And no tricks, or else she dies."

Carsten turned to Fleur. She looked calm, only eyeing the gun pointed at her. "It's gonna be fine," he said. "Look away if you must."

"Looks like your sweetheart's seen the elephant," Eddie said with a cackle as he strode out to the middle of the street.

Carsten stepped into the street and stared Eddie down.

"You had a poor choice of people to love," Eddie said as he took his position. "Miss Fleur's gonna watch you die, knowin' it was her fault."

Carsten held his breath. His eyes narrowed as he stared at Eddie. "Go ahead and draw."

Eddie reached for his gun. Carsten drew his Remington. A gun cracked, its echo resounding through the street. Eddie stood still for a moment, his gun at his side. He dropped to his knees and fell forward.

Carsten turned to face Tucker and McElroy. They gaped at Eddie's body. McElroy fled down the street. Fleur kicked Tucker in the shin and wrenched free of his grip. She ran toward Carsten.

Tucker raised his gun at her. Carsten fired. The man dropped in a heap to the ground.

"Carsten!" Fleur cried out.

He held her close, feeling them both trembling. He ignored the crowd that approached them.

"I'm sorry," she said as tears welled in her eyes. "I got you into this mess. When Morris told me the men who'd kidnapped Attie arrived the ranch, I got scared. I had to find you."

"I know you had to," Carsten said, shedding tears as well. "You did what you felt was right, and there ain't no blame that falls on you. I'm just glad you're safe." He walked over to Eddie's body and kicked dust over him.

"What are you doing?" Fleur asked as she watched him.

"Somethin' Pa told me to do if'n I ever killed someone in a gunfight," he replied. "It's meant to be a show of respect. Come on, let's get out of here." He led Fleur away. As he walked toward the crowd, they gave him a wide berth, allowing him to pass through.

Garrett made his way through the crowd toward them, brandishing his walking stick. "All right, step aside," he said. "What's going on here? Stay away from those bodies. Get an undertaker."

"Gunmen confronted us," Fleur said. "Carsten defended both of us."

"Is that true?" Garrett asked, looking at Carsten.

"That's a fact, Sheriff," Carsten replied. "Three of them. Byron Tucker, Glen McElroy, and Fast Eddie here. Coerced me into a gunfight and threatened Miss Fleur if I didn't do so."

"You were dueling?" Garrett asked as his eyes narrowed. "I don't allow dueling in my county, and that marshal's badge you wear doesn't make you above that law. You're under arrest."

Carsten glared at the sheriff. "It was self-defense and the defense of another," Carsten said. "Plus, one man there is a wanted fugitive."

"I gotta take it up before the judge," Garrett said. "I'm gonna want your gun."

"You'd better take it," Carsten said. His eyes narrowed.

Garrett remained stone-faced. He swung his walking stick. Carsten grabbed the end. In that moment, Garrett grabbed the Remington from Carsten's holster. He cocked the revolver and pointed it at Carsten's midriff.

"I'm pretty fast too," he said, while admiring the gun. "A Remington 1858, new model Army. Cap and ball. Interesting choice of using an antique like that."

"The short barrel's better for a fast draw," Carsten said. "I use the Colt Frontier for range when a Winchester ain't practical. Handy they take the same ammo."

"Speaking of which," Garrett said, gesturing to the Colt in Carsten's other holster. "Take it out and throw it down. Slowly."

Carsten glowered at the sheriff as he complied.

"You and Marshal Cooper both figured I was just another tinhorn, didn't you?" Garrett said.

"Pretty much," Carsten replied with a smirk. "Where is Marshal Cooper, by the by? I can't leave Fleur like this, and someone ought to tell him what happened."

"The Marshal is off duty," Garrett said.

"That means he's roostered in the saloon," Carsten whispered to Fleur.

"Sheriff," she said, standing between the two of them, "I can vouch for Carsten. Eddie challenged him to a showdown and had the others threaten my life if he didn't comply. Carsten shot Eddie and then shot Tucker when he saw he was about to shoot me. He's a hero and doesn't deserve to be arrested. Let him go."

"Get back!" Garrett said as he pointed the revolver at her.

"Drop the guns!" Ross yelled.

Carsten turned around to see the marshal approaching with Ramona and Nash. All had their weapons drawn.

"I thought you were off duty," Carsten remarked.

"When I heard the shots," the marshal replied, "I got the rest of the posse. Figured there'd be a mess, and I'd want numbers for that kinda thing."

"Marshal Cooper," Garrett said with a scowl. "Your deputy was involved in a showdown. You know my policy. I'm takin' him into custody."

"Is that a fact?" Ross asked Carsten.

"Yes, sir," Carsten replied. "I was challenged, and they threatened Fleur at gunpoint. Have you met Fleur Carpentier, by the by?"

"No," Ross said, tipping his hat to Fleur. "Pleasure to make your acquaintance, ma'am."

"Marshal," Fleur said, with a small curtsy. "I just told the sheriff I can vouch for Carsten. He was acting in my defense."

"I don't doubt that," Ross said. "But the sheriff's right. Duelin' is illegal in this county. Carsten, you gotta surrender. I'll make sure you get a lawyer and that Miss Fleur speaks in your defense."

"Much obliged," Carsten said. "Okay then, Sheriff. Take me to jail."

"With pleasure," Garrett replied with a harsh tone. "This way."

Chapter 12
The Trial

The cell in the sheriff's office smelled of filth from the last inmate. Carsten lay back on his cot and stared at the ceiling, wincing as the morning sun shone through the bars.

The door opened. "Hey!" the deputy on duty shouted from the other room, "you got a visitor!"

Carsten groaned. He heaved himself upward and sat up on the cot.

Ross appeared at the cell door, holding a steaming cup of coffee. "Figured you'd want this," he said, passing the cup through the bars.

Carsten stood up and walked to the bars, taking the coffee. He sipped it, feeling energized. "Much obliged," he said as he sat back down. "What's happenin'? Am I headin' to the courthouse?"

"The sheriff will be takin' you there directly," Ross said, "but we got time for a talk."

"Right," Carsten said, scratching his back. "Is Fleur okay?"

"I put her in a hotel while we wait for your trial," Ross said. "She'll be safe."

"Much obliged," Carsten replied. "So, what do you need to talk about with me?"

"Well, I wired the sheriff in Yuma County," Ross said as he leaned back against the wall. "He says there was a riot in Yuma Territorial Prison a couple weeks back, and two inmates escaped. Byron Tucker and Glen McElroy."

"Yup," Carsten said. "Fleur told me they'd come by my family's ranch. That's why she's in Phoenix right now. Tucker's dead, but McElroy got away since the sheriff seemed more interested in takin' me in."

"We can worry 'bout that when the trial's over," Ross said. "But I was thinkin' 'bout what we was discussin' earlier. Garrett rarely gives me or any of my people this much trouble. I reckon he suspects somethin'."

"I did see him twitch when I mentioned el Presidente," Carsten said, stroking his chin. "I definitely underestimated him when he disarmed me, but I reckon he might be hidin' somethin'."

"What do you reckon?" Ross asked.

"Not much right now," Carsten replied as he paced up and down his cell. "I'm wonderin' if Garrett knows somethin' 'bout el Presidente he don't want us knowin'?"

"Keep talkin'," Ross said.

"I thought Wiley's stories 'bout el Presidente were just tall yarns," Carsten said, stretching his arms behind his head. "That sniper seemed to be gunnin' for Wiley, and when I caught him, he mentioned he was a traitor. I reckon el Presidente was the one who hired the sniper, but I wonder what Wiley did to rile the elusive big bug."

"That we know already," Ross said. "But where does the sheriff fit in?"

Carsten downed the contents of his coffee cup and placed it on the cot beside him. "Well," he said as put his hands together in contemplation, "he seemed so adamant in bringin' me in after I mentioned el Presidente. I reckon he's gonna be aimin' to get the book thrown at me in the courthouse today. Clearly I know too much, and he wants to silence me. That showdown just gave him an excuse. I reckon he's involved with el Presidente in some way. Why else would he still be pressin' charges?"

"If that's the case," Ross said, "we'd best be on guard."

As Carsten nodded in agreement, the door opened again. An old, bespectacled man in a black suit and Kentucky tie entered the cell. "Carsten McNeil?" he asked, looking over a set of notes.

"Yes, I'm Carsten McNeil," Carsten replied.

"Excellent," the man said, extending his hand. "I'm Ambrose Cunningham. I'll be your attorney."

"What are my chances?" Carsten asked as he shook the lawyer's hand.

"Miss Carpentier's testimony should exonerate you without a problem," Ambrose replied. "You have a strong case with the self-defense plea."

"Well, are we ready?" Carsten asked.

***

Carsten said nothing as he sat at the defendant's table with Ambrose. The crowded gallery worsened the lingering stench of sweat and body odor. He looked over at the plaintiff's table, where Sheriff Garrett sat with a younger attorney.

He leaned over to Ambrose. "You recognize the lawyer?" he whispered.

"Reed Kirkham," Ambrose replied. "Some rising star in the circuit courts. That sheriff must really have it in for you to be pressin' charges."

"All rise for Judge Moses Day!" the bailiff called.

Carsten stood up.

A stern-looking man with a gray moustache took his seat at the bench. "Carsten McNeil," he said. "You are charged with the fatal shooting of Edward Morley in a gunfight along with that of Byron Tucker. How do you plead?"

"Not guilty, your honor."

"As you wish," the judge said. "Mr. Kirkham, if you will."

"Thank you, your honor," Kirkham said as he stood up. "I would like to present my witness for the prosecution, Sheriff John Garrett of Maricopa County."

Garrett walked to the witness chair, swearing an oath when presented with a Bible by the bailiff.

"Mr. Garrett," Kirkham said, "can you tell us about the events of yesterday?"

"Mr. McNeil returned to Phoenix as part of a federal posse led by U.S. Marshal Ross Cooper," he said. "They had apprehended the wanted outlaw, Wiley Frye, and several members of his gang, and I invited Marshal Cooper and Deputy McNeil to have a drink to celebrate the arrests. Carsten declined the invitation and went to meet someone at the train station while Marshal Cooper and I went to the saloon. When I heard shooting in the station's direction, I ran there and found Mr. McNeil had shot two men in what appeared to be a showdown. I attempted to take him into custody, and he tried to resist."

"You went straight to the station to apprehend him?" Kirkham asked.

"I did."

"What about Marshal Cooper?"

"He went off to get reinforcements. He convinced Carsten to surrender."

"You may ask, Mr. Cunningham," Kirkham said, returning to his table.

Ambrose stood up and approached the sheriff. "Mr. Garrett," he began, "are you aware of the identities of the deceased?"

"Objection!" Kirkham shouted. "Relevance."

"I'm trying to find out how the events came to pass, your honor," Ambrose replied.

"Objection overruled," the judge said. "Proceed, counselor."

"As Sheriff of Maricopa County, did the deceased have any outstanding warrants for county matters?"

"They did not," Garrett said.

"According to statements by U.S. Marshal Ross Cooper," Ambrose said, "the first deceased victim, Edward Morley, was known throughout the territory as Fast Eddie, with warrants for murder in Texas and the New Mexico Territory. The second victim, Byron Tucker, had been convicted of destruction of property and an accessory to the kidnapping of Attie McNeil, the defendant's sister. He and an accomplice, Glen McElroy, were reported as having escaped from Yuma Territorial Prison. Were you aware of those facts?"

"I was not," Garrett said. He exchanged an uncomfortable glance with Kirkham.

"Were you made aware by U.S. Marshal Cooper or the defendant?"

"Carsten stated one victim was a fugitive from justice."

"Thank you Mr. Garrett," Ambrose said. "No further questions."

Garrett returned to his table.

"Your honor," Ambrose said to the judge, "I'd like to present a case that my client was acting in self-defense and the defense of another. I'd like to call my witness, Miss Fleur Carpentier."

Carsten smiled as Fleur swore the oath and sat in the witness chair.

"Miss Carpentier," Ambrose said, "can you tell the jury how you know the defendant?"

"Carsten and his family were regular customers at my father's general store in Cripple Gorge in Yavapai County," she said. "Last year, we entered a relationship."

"And were you able to identify any of the victims?"

"Fast Eddie had confronted Carsten and his father in our family's store last year," she said. "During a scuffle, Fast Eddie challenged Carsten to a gunfight, who won the draw and shot him in the hand. As for Tucker and McElroy, they worked for a man named Alphonse Moraday, who had been seeking to purchase the businesses in and around Cripple Gorge. They kidnapped Carsten's sister when his family refused to sell their ranch."

"And can you tell us about the events that transpired?" Ambrose asked.

"I traveled to Phoenix to see Carsten, where we were confronted by Eddie, Tucker, and another man named McElroy. Eddie demanded Carsten face him in a showdown right then, and his friends threatened my life if he refused. Tucker held me hostage but I managed to escape when Carsten shot Eddie. He then shot Tucker when he tried to shoot me."

"And what about McElroy?"

"He ran away while Carsten was seeing to me," Fleur replied, smiling at Carsten. "After all, he was off duty."

"You may ask, Mr. Kirkham," Ambrose said as he sat down.

"Miss Carpentier," Kirkham asked, "what was your purpose for traveling to Phoenix? Was it arranged by you and Carsten?"

"Tucker and McElroy had visited the McNeil family ranch seeking Carsten's whereabouts," she replied. "I had come to Phoenix to warn him they were looking for revenge. They admitted they had followed me when they confronted us."

"Did you believe your life was in danger?" Kirkham asked.

Fleur gave him a look of disbelief. "Yes," she said in a stern tone. "Tucker had a loaded gun pointed to my head that was cocked."

"Have you traveled with Carsten before?" he asked. "Is it true you rode with him in a raid on a ranch owed by Mr. Moraday?"

"Objection!" Ambrose called out. "Leading."

"Sustained," the judge said.

"Have you accompanied Carsten on any previous ventures?"

"I helped him rescue his sister from Alphonse Moraday," she said.

***

The clock in the courtroom ticked away as Ross took his seat in the witness chair.

"Carsten McNeil has served under me as a U.S. Deputy Marshal for just over a year," he said. "In all that time, he has always been reluctant to kill, even in the line of duty, and shot nobody except in self-defense or the defense of others. Despite that reluctance, he has distinguished himself as an exceptional lawman, like his daddy before him."

"Is it true that prior to his swearing to uphold the law, the defendant was responsible for the killings of Alphonse Moraday and William Harvey the previous year?" Kirkham asked.

"That is true," Ross said, staring the prosecutor down. "But like today, Carsten was acting in the defense of his sister, whom Moraday had kidnapped. William Harvey, known throughout the territory as English Bill, was an accomplice."

***

Carsten fidgeted as he saw the jurors return to the courtroom. He heard his heart beating as he contemplated their verdict.

"Members of the jury," the judge said, "how do you find the accused?"

"Your honor," one juror said, "we believe Carsten was acting in self-defense in a gunfight he himself did not start and accepted under duress. He also acted valiantly in defending Miss Carpentier, and therefore, we find him not guilty."

Carsten felt a sense of relief as the words resounded through the courtroom. He shook his attorney's hand. As he looked over at Garrett, he saw the sheriff fuming as he stared at him.

"Deputy McNeil," the judge said, "you may leave this court a free man. Your effects will be returned to you. And I commend your ongoing service to the Arizona Territory in your capacity as a deputy marshal."

"Thank you, your honor," Carsten replied.

"Sheriff Garrett," the judge said, turning to the sheriff, "might I suggest you think twice before wasting this court's time by attempting to bring up charges against a fellow lawman. I don't care what petty squabble you have with Deputy McNeil, but if you involve me in such an incident again, you will be in contempt. Is that understood?"

"Yes, your honor," Garrett replied with his head bowed.

Carsten stepped outside the courtroom with Ross. Fleur was waiting for him, and he hugged her.

"I'm so glad they acquitted you," she said. "Now, can we go home?"

"I reckon so," Carsten replied. He looked at Ross for approval.

"You go on now," he said with a proud smile. "Your work here's done till Wiley gets tried, and you could use a break. Next train to Prescott's early tomorrow, so you'd best find a hotel."

"Much obliged," Carsten said, tipping his hat. "I reckon Fleur and me ought to have dinner for two while we're here."

"Yes, well done today," Garrett said as he appeared behind Carsten. "If I were you, I wouldn't stay here much longer. This city can be quite dangerous for up-and-coming gunfighters."

Carsten remained stone-faced as the sheriff stared him down. He felt Fleur's grip tighten around his hand as he watched the sheriff stride away.

"I don't like this," Fleur said. "There's something sinister about that sheriff."

"Agreed," Ross said. "Carsten and I spoke 'bout this before the trial. You'd best head off. I'll look into this. Garrett is hidin' somethin', and I'm gonna find out what."

Chapter 13
A Thief in the Night

Sweat poured down McElroy's face as he hid in the alleyway. His legs still ached from when he'd fled the station as Carsten shot Eddie and Tucker. He pressed against the wall when he heard footsteps and talking draw near. A couple passed the alleyway without stopping. McElroy exhaled as the sound drew further away. He peered out of the alleyway, seeing the shadows cast by the early evening sun. He planned to leave at nightfall, so he sat down on an overturned box, his stomach rumbling.

As McElroy stared at the floor, he noticed a wad of bills land by his feet. He kneeled down to pick it up and heard a clicking sound. He felt something metal press against his head.

"Stay right there," a commanding voice said. "If you so much as glance upward, I'll blow your brains out."

"Who are you?" McElroy asked, his voice cracking as he spoke.

"I am el Presidente," the unseen man said. "And I know who you are, Glen McElroy."

McElroy swallowed as he heard his name.

"I hear you have a grudge against Carsten McNeil. That he killed two of your companions today."

"Forget that," McElroy said. "I don't want nothin' to do with that no more. If I face him in a showdown, I'm a dead man. I'm gettin' outta this town. Find some work elsewhere. Maybe south of the border."

"Another showdown is unnecessary," el Presidente replied. "Marshal Cooper is looking into my affairs. He and Carsten know too much, so I have a plan to deal with them both. Help me, and you'll be able to leave town unmolested. Does that sound like a deal to your liking?"

McElroy gave a curt nod, keeping his focus on the dollar bills on the floor while trying to avoid looking up.

"If they blame Carsten for Ross Cooper's death, it will give you time to get out. Carsten's staying at the Golden Brook Hotel, but he's leaving town in the morning, so hurry. Marshal Cooper frequents the Old Hunter Saloon. There aren't many gunfighters around here who use a cap and ball Remington, if you get my meaning."

"Sneak into Carsten's hotel room, steal his Remington, and use it to kill the marshal?" McElroy said. "I think I'm cottoning on to what you're saying."

"So you'll do it?"

"A heroic deputy shootin' his boss and gettin' hanged for it?" McElroy asked. "I'd love to see that."

"Consider that money a parting gift," el Presidente said. "I trust a scofflaw like you know how to pick locks?"

"Yes," McElroy replied. A small leather pouch landed by his feet. McElroy felt the gun barrel removed from his head as he grabbed the money and the pouch.

He looked up, and the alleyway was empty so he sat back down on the box and opened the pouch, finding a set of lock picks inside. He pocketed the pouch and counted the money.

"A hundred dollars…" he muttered to himself as he finished counting. "That's more than Big Al ever paid."

***

The lobby of the Golden Brook Hotel carried an overpowering scent of floor polish. McElroy held his breath as he walked toward the front desk.

A well-dressed manager looked him over. "How may I help you, sir?" he asked.

"I'd like a room, please." McElroy said. "Just for two nights. I'm passing through."

"Of course," the manager replied, producing a registry book from behind the desk. "If you'd like to sign the register. It's two dollars a night." He handed McElroy a pencil and opened the book.

McElroy signed the entry as B. Jones. He scanned across the other entries, noticing Carsten's and Fleur's names and room numbers in the entry above him. He gave a brief smirk as he made a mental note. He returned the pencil to the manager as he handed him a five-dollar bill. "Keep the change," he said.

"Enjoy your stay, Mr. Jones," the manager replied as he handed him a key.

***

Night fell. McElroy peered out of his room. Seeing nobody in the hallway, he crept out, his boots in his hands while his bare feet touched the carpet that ran down the hallway. He shuffled along, making as little noise as possible. When he reached Carsten's room at the end of the hall, he kneeled by the door and pressed his ear against the wood. He heard no sounds within. He produced the lock picks and began to work. A bead of sweat ran down his forehead as he listened to the tumblers move, hoping they weren't too audible. He tried the doorknob, and the door pushed open.

A small window was open at the end of the room, providing a gentle breeze that did little to ease the heat. McElroy crawled inside. He felt around on the floor, finding a pile of clothes near Carsten's bed. Moving his hands through the pile, he tried to discern any leather. Nothing. He crept toward the bed. He reached out for the frame at the head, freezing as he felt Carsten's breath on him.

Wood gave way to leather as he discerned Carsten's gun belt hanging from one of the bed posts, allowing him to reach his gun from where he lay. Probing further, McElroy found the pistol's grip and lifted it out of the holster. He was creeping away when a floorboard creaked. McElroy froze.

Carsten stirred for a moment but didn't wake.

McElroy wiped the sweat from his forehead and left the room, closing the door behind him.

***

The cool breeze provided more relief outdoors than indoors as McElroy made his way down the deserted streets of Phoenix. Most businesses and storefronts had closed, and many saloons had quieted down.

As he approached the Old Hunter Saloon, he heard drunken singing. A figure lumbered down the street, bottle of whiskey in hand while butchering a trail song too incoherently for McElroy to recognize. He walked closer, trying to discern the man while reeling back at the powerful smell of whiskey on his breath. In the moonlight, he barely recognized the face of Marshal Cooper.

He walked past the drunk man, hoping he hadn't been recognized either. McElroy stopped once the man passed. He pulled back the hammer of Carsten's Remington. The drunken singing continued. He turned around and raised the revolver, aiming it at Ross's back. He pulled the trigger. The singing stopped as Ross slumped forward. McElroy fired again and again until the hammer fell on an empty chamber. He dropped the revolver and fled into the nearby alley as people flocked out to the street in response to the shooting.

"It's the marshal!" he heard someone shout. "And he's been shot in the back! Someone get the sheriff!"

"Look!" someone else said. "I've found a gun! The killer must've dropped it 'fore he lit out!"

"Let's see!" a third voice said. "A Remington 1858? I ain't seen a shootin' iron like that in a while. If'n I do, they're converted to cartridges."

"I know a fella who uses a Remington," the second voice said. "Carsten McNeil favors one for the quick draw."

A sly grin came to McElroy's lips as he heard Carsten's name.

Chapter 14
Carsten-the Fugitive

The following morning, Carsten woke up with a stir. As he eased himself out of bed, he noticed his Remington missing from his holster. He looked underneath the bed, finding nothing except the chamber pot. He scratched his head, wondering where the gun would have fallen. A gentle tapping on the door prompted him to freeze.

"Carsten?" Fleur's voice sounded behind the door. "Are you ready for breakfast? We need to be at the station soon."

"I'll be out directly," he replied. "Just let me get outta my long-Johns and into some regular duds." After getting changed, Carsten opened the door. He tensed—it had been unlocked.

Fleur entered and kissed him on the cheek. "You hungry?" she asked.

"Famished," Carsten replied in a noncommittal tone.

"You okay?" she asked.

"I think someone's been in my room," he said. "My door's been unlocked, and I lost my Remington."

"Did you check under the bed?" she asked. "It could have fallen out."

"That was the first place I looked," Carsten replied. "Somethin' ain't right."

Fleur opened her mouth to speak but was interrupted by the sound of booted feet tromping up the stairs.

Carsten gripped Fleur's hand as he saw Sheriff Garrett appear in the corridor. Nash and Ramona flanked him, both with revolvers drawn.

"Sheriff Garrett?" Carsten asked. "What's goin' on?"

"Carsten McNeil," he said, "you're under arrest for the murder of U.S. Marshal Ross Cooper. I'm here to disarm you. Throw up your hands."

"But I was here all night," Carsten replied. "Fleur can vouch for me."

"I'm sure," Garrett replied. "But can you explain how Marshal Cooper was found dead in front of the Old Hunter Saloon, shot in the back with this weapon found at the scene?" He produced Carsten's Remington. "You may have escaped justice for dueling Fast Eddie, but you'll hang for this."

Carsten shoved Garrett back into Nash and Ramona.

"In here, quick!" Fleur said, pulling his arm.

Carsten followed her into her room, slamming the door behind him. He pushed the wardrobe over so it blocked the door. Loud banging echoed throughout the room. Fleur pointed to the window. Carsten nodded in agreement. He climbed through onto the porch roof.

"Go," she said. "I can claim you took me hostage and forced me to help you."

"I can't do that," Carsten replied, shaking his head. "They'll see right through it."

He pulled Fleur through the window as the banging on the door gave way to the sound of wood cracking. "Let's go," Carsten said. He ran across the porch roof with Fleur and leaped into a pile of refuse in the back alley. He gagged at the smell, and Fleur tried to brush garbage off her dress.

"Where do we go from here?" she asked.

"The livery," Carsten replied as he ran down the alleyway. "We need to get our horses."

"I don't have a horse," Fleur said.

"I brought a packhorse," Carsten replied. "If I dump his gear, you can ride him." He peered out of the alleyway onto the next street.

A few townspeople and the occasional rider passed by. He nodded to Fleur. The pair ran across the street down to the next alleyway. Carsten panted as he leaned against a wall.

"What about the station?" Fleur asked. "We could ride the train back to Prescott."

"That ain't gonna work," Carsten said. "I've just been accused of killin' my boss, who was the marshal for the whole territory. I'm gonna be the most wanted man in Arizona in short order. We need to get the horses, hide out somewhere until dark, and then get outta here."

"So where do we hide?" Fleur asked, looking around.

"We'll find somewhere close to the livery," Carsten replied. "Let's hope they ain't watchin' the place."

Carsten led Fleur to a wagon builder's yard on Cortez Street. He peered over the wall. A few stagecoaches and wagons in various stages of completion sat on the opposite side. No sign of any workers. He straddled the wall, helping

Fleur over. He pointed to the nearest covered wagon and helped her inside.

As she sat down, Fleur exhaled. "Okay," she said, "where do we go from here? What's going on? Why would you kill the marshal?"

Carsten said nothing, peering out of the wagon.

"I'm sorry," she continued. "I'm asking too many questions, but I'm just a little shook right now."

"It's fine," Carsten replied, holding her hand. "It's a long story, and it involves some kinda boogeyman who goes by the handle of el Presidente."

"A boogeyman?" Flora said, cracking a smile.

"I didn't believe it either," Carsten replied, "but the last couple days have left me wonderin' 'bout things. I first heard 'bout the fella from an outlaw we arrested named Wiley Frye. Someone who's demandin' tribute from all the bandits in this territory. Well, it seems this fella has it in for Mr. Frye since he sent some sharpshooter to try to bushwhack him on the way back to Phoenix."

"And where does the sheriff fit in this?" Fleur asked.

"Well, he seemed adamant in bringin' me to justice after I discussed it with him," Carsten said. "So I reckon he's involved somehow. Marshal Cooper probably stumbled upon somethin' he shouldn't have, and if I get the blame for his killin' and am given a hemp necktie, then this Presidente fella can keep runnin' his little operation with nobody else figurin' it out."

"So you can't just turn yourself in and ride the trial?" Fleur asked.

"No," Carsten said. "I need to get you back to Cripple Gorge. Your pa's gonna be worried somethin' fierce if'n the word gets back to him."

"I'm staying with you," Fleur said. "They'll probably target me if I leave. I helped you rescue your sister from Big Al. I'm sure I can help you clear your name."

"Clear my name?" Carsten asked. "How do I do that? I'd need to find someone who knows 'bout el Presidente's organization." He paused.

"What's wrong?" Fleur said.

"Oh…" Carsten mumbled in realization. "We gotta head to the marshal's office. We gotta speak to Wiley Frye."

"What makes you think he'll talk if he hasn't already?" Fleur asked, raising an eyebrow.

"Because I'm the only one who'll believe him right now, and we have to spring him. We're outlaws now, and I reckon we'll need to ride the river with someone who knows how to live outside the law."

***

As night fell, Carsten and Fleur hid in an alleyway near the marshal's office. Nobody roamed the streets.

"Are you sure about this?" Fleur asked.

"I really ain't," Carsten replied, "but we have little choice right now."

The couple walked across the street toward the building. Carsten peered through the window. He noticed one deputy, asleep in his chair with his feet resting on the desk. A lamp sat at the opposite end of the desk.

Carsten turned to Fleur and put his finger to his lips. He eased his Colt Frontier out of its holster and crept inside the office. Once inside, Carsten could hear the deputy's snoring. He waved for Fleur to enter as he looked toward the holding cells, not noticeable from outside.

Wiley sat in one cell, chained to the floor by his ankle. He looked up and saw Carsten enter. "What do you want?" he asked, giving the question some volume.

The deputy woke as he heard Wiley's voice, falling backward on his chair. Seeing Carsten, he scrambled for the revolver in his holster.

Carsten aimed his Colt Frontier and thumbed back the hammer with an audible click. "I don't wanna do this. You can walk away if'n you stay calm."

The deputy nodded, raising his hands.

Fleur entered, closing and bolting the door behind her. As she picked up the overturned chair, Carsten gestured for the deputy to sit down. Fleur grabbed the gun from the deputy's holster and trained it on him. Carsten grabbed a coil of rope hanging from the wall and tied him to the chair.

"You ain't gonna get away with this, McNeil," the deputy said. "Garrett and Nash are lookin' for you. They got deputies waitin' at the livery and the station. You're gonna hang for killin' the marshal."

"I didn't kill Marshal Cooper," Carsten replied, grabbing a stained handkerchief from the deputy's vest pocket and stuffing it in his mouth before securing it with a spare bandana. "I can't prove it if I turn myself in. Now you're gonna keep quiet while I speak to Mr. Frye."

"Huh?" Wiley said as he heard his name being mentioned. "If you wanna join my gang, you're a little late. Those still breathin' got carted off to Yuma."

"Who's el Presidente?" Carsten asked as he rummaged for the keys.

"Straight to the point," Wiley said. "You ain't as conversational as you were last time we met. Who's the lady?"

"This here's my current partner, Fleur Carpentier," Carsten said. "Fleur, this is Wiley Frye, a notorious outlaw."

Fleur gave Wiley a curt nod.

"So you're wantin' to try the life of an outlaw?" Wiley asked. "What's in it for me? You need my help, and that ain't a question. You're gonna offer a lighter sentence if I talk, but I know you're wanted, so that ain't gonna slide."

Carsten opened his mouth to speak but said nothing.

"He's got you there," Fleur remarked. "Just get him out so we can find a way out of here."

"El Presidente ordered the killin' of my boss," Carsten replied as he rattled a ring of keys. "And you're the only one I can ask since you mentioned him. I'm gonna be breakin' ya out, since I need someone who operates outside the law and has some knowledge of el Presidente's gang. We have a deal?"

Wiley laughed. "You drive a hard bargain. Fine. You get me out, and I'll tell you what I know once I'm outta here."

"Hey!" Fleur hissed as she looked through the window. "I think we've got company."

Carsten peered over to the window and saw torches outside. Sheriff Garrett waited on horseback outside the office, along with Nash and Ramona. Several other deputies flanked them with rifles trained on the door.

"McNeil!" Garrett shouted. "We know you're in there! You thought Marshal Nash and I wouldn't figure out you'd go after Wiley? Well, you figured wrong. Come on out with your hands up!"

"Great…" Carsten hissed. "Now what?"

"I'm waitin' on your answer," Wiley said.

Carsten threw the keys to Fleur, who ran over and unlocked the cell. "How did you figure that out?" he called to Garrett. "You've been wantin' to get rid of me since I mentioned el Presidente. What are you hidin'?"

"It's your word against mine about conspiracies like that," Garrett said, "but I have the weapon that proves you killed Marshal Cooper. It'll look a lot better for you at your trial if you cooperate now."

Carsten said nothing. A whistle from inside attracted his attention. He turned to face Wiley and Fleur.

Wiley held out a stick of dynamite. "Must have been left over from an old case," he said.

"It's crowded at the front door," Carsten said, "so we'll leave through the back."

Wiley cracked a smile at the remark. He placed the stick of dynamite by the wall in the cell and lit it. Carsten shoved the deputy to the ground while Fleur and Wiley overturned the desk.

"Sounds like you're getting ready for a siege!" Garrett called from outside. "If you don't come out, I'll have no choice but to smoke you out."

"Go right ahead," Carsten mumbled to himself. He ducked behind the desk and stuck his fingers in his ears.

The explosion resounded across the street. Dust from the masonry filled the room. Carsten choked as he ventured through the cloud, discerning the hole in the cell wall. He made out Wiley's form running through the gap and, grabbing Fleur, ran after him.

***

After a convoluted journey through the back streets and alleys of Phoenix, Carsten and his friends reached the livery where he had stabled Dan and Bill. Many people were running through the streets toward the marshal's office.

"Good thinkin' with the dynamite there," Wiley said with a smirk. "I reckon we woke the entire city up."

"I'll apologize to them later," Carsten replied. "I reckon that'll include deputies watchin' the livery."

"Let's not hang around and find out," Wiley said, pushing his way past Carsten.

Carsten followed Wiley as he wrenched the bar off the livery doors. The smell of horses and straw greeted him. He made his way down the stalls to find Dan and Bill.

"Hey, what are you doing here?" a voice said behind them.

Carsten turned around.

A man approached him with a bullseye lantern hanging off the end of a shotgun.

"Just collecting my horses," Carsten said, gesturing for Fleur to get behind him. "I got the paperwork to prove it."

"We're closed," the watchman said, thumbing back the hammers of his shotgun.

"I'm in a hurry," Carsten said.

As the watchman approached, Wiley emerged from behind another stall. He tapped the watchman on the shoulder and floored him with a punch to the face. He grabbed the shotgun as the man fell. "Are we ready to leave?" he asked, saddling another horse.

"What are you doing?" Carsten hissed as he watched him.

"Borrowin' this horse," Wiley replied. "Mine's dead, remember."

"They still hang horse thieves," Carsten said. "I don't want no part in that."

"Well, you ain't got much choice in that," Wiley said. "But we ain't got time to argue."

Carsten produced some money and dropped it on the ground near the watchman. He grabbed his saddle and cinched it to Dan, leading him out with Bill.

"Leave that junk," Wiley said, undoing the saddlebags on Bill and sending them to the floor with a clatter.

"Hey!" Carsten said. "Don't we need that out in the wilderness?"

"He can't carry all that and your sweetheart there," Wiley replied. He took another saddle and fastened it.

"Thank you," Fleur said as she mounted. She flicked the reins and led the horse out the gate.

Carsten and Wiley followed her. Outside, Carsten rode after Fleur at a trot.

"We'd best pony up and make ourselves scarce," Wiley said, flicking his reins and loping ahead. "Try to keep up."

Carsten shrugged. He and Fleur loped after him out of Phoenix.

Chapter 15
The Hunt Begins

McElroy pulls his hat low as he leaves the hotel the following morning. Stepping outside, he hears a rifle being cocked. He raises his hands as a Mexican woman in a long duster and wide-brimmed hat jabbs him in the cheek with a Winchester.

"Glen McElroy," she said, "you escaped from Yuma Territorial Prison over two weeks ago."

"I'm sorry, señorita," he replied, "but you must have me mistaken for someone else. My handle's Jones." He felt the barrel come away from his cheek as he exhaled, only to feel the butt of the rifle hit him in the stomach. He doubled over.

"Don't play games with me, cabrón," she said. "The warrant states dead or alive, and I don't have to feed the latter when I transport one."

McElroy retched and looked up. "I know you," he said in a quiet voice. "You're that bounty hunter, Ramona Vasquez. Okay, I'll come with you."

"Not so fast, Ramona," a familiar voice said. A well-dressed man walked toward them, accompanied by a drab-looking one carrying a Bible.

"Sheriff Garrett," Ramona said. "And Deputy Nash. Which of you wants this man?"

"If he's wanted in Yuma County," Garrett said, "then it's none of my business, since it isn't a county matter. But this man is small fry compared to our plans."

"Plans?" Ramona said, keeping her rifle trained on McElroy.

"With Marshal Cooper's passing," Garrett continued, "Mr. Nash here has stepped up as the acting marshal for the Arizona Territory. His first bid is to pursue Carsten McNeil and Wiley Frye. Would you care to join him?"

"You're goin' after Quaker McNeil?" McElroy asked. "I can help you with that."

"Silence!" Nash growled at him.

"Just one moment, Marshal," Garrett said, raising his hand. "Let's hear what this fellow has to say." The sheriff helped McElroy to his feet.

"Much obliged," McElroy said, tipping his hat. "Carsten's family has a ranch in Yavapai County near Cripple Gorge. I reckon we wait for him there."

"We?" Garrett said with a chuckle. "What makes you think 'we' are going after him?"

"I used to work on the neighborin' ranch," McElroy said, "so I know where it's located. You put in a good word with the judge for me, and I'll lead you there myself."

A silence followed. Ramona and Garrett exchanged glances while Nash continued to scowl at McElroy. He smiled at the marshal, whose expression remained unchanged.

"What about my bounty?" Ramona said. "The reward for Carsten had better be bigger."

"Love of money is the root of all evil," Nash said.

"I don't work for free, padre." Ramona glowered at him. "This hombre is wanted dead or alive, so you can either stop preaching for five minutes to give me an answer, or I'll put a bullet in him and claim that reward."

"The reward is five hundred dollars for Carsten," Garrett said, tapping his walking stick on the ground.

"And I don't want the money," McElroy replied, sweat pouring down his face. "I'm helpin' you if you help me in return. After all, ain't there somethin' in that Good Book of yours 'bout settin' a thief to catch a thief?"

"No," Nash said in a stern tone.

"Well, the sentiment's there," McElroy said.

"He has a point," Ramona said. "When Carsten goes home, we can apprehend him real easy. If he ain't home, we can wait for him. And if his family try to go after him, we can follow 'em."

"Yeah, see?" McElroy said, pointing at her and nodding.

"Fine," Nash said.

McElroy rubbed his hands in anticipation, but Ramona grabbed him by the shirt collar. "I'm only doin' this 'cause Carsten's worth more than you are," she said to him. "But if you're wrong, or you try anything, I'll shoot you myself. And it'll be slow. Understood?"

McElroy gave a hasty nod.

"We must raise our posse," Nash said. "Seek the path of the righteous man."

"Agreed," Garrett said. "I, meanwhile, will lead my own posse to apprehend him before he leaves the county."

Chapter 16
Going to Ground

Carsten's eyes felt heavy as he watched the morning sunrise. He and his companions walked their horses down the Apache Trail toward the Gila River.

"We'll stop here," Wiley said. "Our horses will need to rest for a spell."

Carsten heaved himself out of his saddle. He patted Dan's mane as the horse ate some nearby grass. Sitting on the riverbank, he splashed water on his face.

Wiley wade into the river and bent down, holding his hands out as if he were going to clap. He smacked his hands in the water. His hands emerged with a wriggling fish. "Make yourself useful, will you?" Wiley said as he tossed the fish to the bank. "Find somethin' to make a fire with. Quicker we do that, quicker we can move on. It ain't a good idea to stay too long in one place."

***

The smell of fish lingered with the smoke on the cooking fire. Flies swarmed the remains of their breakfast.

"So," Fleur asked, "where are we heading?"

"I think we ought to head home," Carsten said. "The sheriff in Prescott might buy our story. He's an old friend of me and my pa."

"You head to the sheriff, and you'll be walkin' into a hangman's noose," Wiley said as he took a drink from his canteen. "I didn't wanna mention this back at the livery, but you can't afford to balk at breakin' the law. You saw the hand, you gotta play the hand." He stood up and walked to the river to fill his canteen.

"Perhaps you can tell him of el Presidente," Fleur said. "What's his beef with you, anyway?"

Wiley sat down on the bank, gazing into the ripples on the water. "I got greedy," he said. "This fella gave me and my boys a tip 'bout some real lucrative hauls, whether banks, trains, or stagecoaches. I took him up on the offer, and he wanted a cut in return while takin' care of the law. But the info wasn't always accurate. Other gangs got there first. Hauls weren't as big as he'd advertised. My boys got killed. But he still wanted his cut, and that was always the lion's share of the profits. I decided I was gonna keep the money on our last job. Take it and run without payin' him the tribute. But we found the law, and we found bounty hunters. We spent most of the haul on supplies and went to ground in the mountains. Then you showed up."

Carsten moved next to Wiley and patted him on the shoulder. "If'n you tell the sheriff who el Presidente is, you might save your hide and mine."

"You're bargainin' still needs work," Wiley said. "I'm only helpin' you since you helped me. But even if I say who el

Presidente is, I'm still wanted for many things. I'll still have people comin' after me for the price on my head."

"Well," Carsten replied, "I won't be one of them."

"That's real comfortin', kid," Wiley said in a sarcastic tone. "But I already told you, I never met el Presidente."

"What?" Fleur said as she loomed over him. "Then you led us out here for nothing? Is he even real?"

"I didn't say he ain't real," Wiley replied. "I said I never met him in person. Everythin' was done through dead drops. But I reckon you might know who he could be." He stared at Carsten, who fidgeted for a moment.

"Garrett," Carsten said with a snap of his fingers. "He sent me and the marshal after you and was quite specific on that front. Then he got me arrested for that showdown. I'd mentioned el Presidente to him, and he seemed to laugh that off. But then he arrested me after that duel. When that failed, he probably killed the marshal... or at least ordered it."

"But how do we prove it?"

"Great..." Carsten said. "That don't help us one bit." He stood up and threw a stone downstream.

Fleur walked up and put a hand on his shoulder. "Maybe we need to think about leaving. And I want you to know that, wherever you go, I'd like to go with you."

"Thanks," Carsten replied, resting his hand on hers.

"If we can't go home, where can we go?" she said.

"Mexico," Wiley replied. "We'll head south of the border. That'll keep the marshals away. We'll find sanctuary someplace down there, but it'll probably cost us somethin' fierce. You ready to make a quick buck?"

"No!" Carsten snapped, raising his hand. "I ain't turnin' into no robber."

"You've seen the hand," Wiley reminded him. "You gotta play it."

Carsten stared Wiley down. He slid his Colt Frontier from his holster and cocked it. "I ain't like you," he said. "I've never run in my life. If'n I don't clear this up, I'll never see my family again. I'm gonna prove Garrett is a criminal and I'm innocent, then I'm gonna throw the law he's abusin' against him. I helped spring you 'cause I figured you'd have answers. But it looks like you don't. I'll hang if I try to turn you in, so if you can't help me, I'll leave you to the vultures."

Everyone fell silent.

Wiley gave a slow clap. "Maybe you will get by on the wrong side of the law. But you kill me, then you and the pretty Miss Fleur will be on your lonesome in handlin' this. You'll need somewhere to hide and I know the perfect place."

"Where?" Fleur asked.

"My cousin Don owns a saloon near Tucson," Wiley said. "Rowdy place. No lawmen will go near it. They call the place From Dusk Till Don's."

"We'd best mount up," Carsten said, noticing trail dust from a large group of riders on the horizon. "It'll be at least four days' ride to Tucson. Longer since we got a posse or two on our tail."

"Let's hope that's a county posse," Wiley replied. "They won't chase us far."

Chapter 17
Big Brother Instinct

A day later, Morris wiped the sweat from his brow as he led his horse to the barn. He removed his saddle and carried it over to the corral. As he hung it on the fence, he watched the sunset.

"Another day, another dollar," Davey remarked as he sat in the shade provided by the barn.

"Yup," Morris said, noting a dust cloud on the trail.

"Morris!" Attie shouted. "It looks like company!"

Morris discerned a group of riders approaching the yard. "They're off the main trail," he said. "It don't look good. Everyone get inside!" Morris grabbed his Henry rifle from its saddle ring and ran inside the house, ignoring the smell of the bean casserole.

Vince was stirring the cooking pot while Cassie set the table.

"No running in the house," Cassie said, placing her hands on her hips.

"We got riders comin'," Morris replied. "Close the windows." He stood by the door as the riders loped into the yard. He counted at least five, recognizing one of them as McElroy. "Attie," he said, "stay down."

"Why?" his sister replied.

"Let me do the talkin'," Morris said. "If shootin' starts, you'll have more cover indoors." He gripped his rifle and stepped outside. "That's far enough," he said. "Now you'd best state your business."

A stern-faced man in a plain black outfit trotted forward. As he drew closer, Morris noticed a badge on his lapel. "Is this the McNeil Ranch?" he asked.

"It is," Morris said. "If you're lookin' for my brother, he's with a posse down in Phoenix. Who wants to know anyhow?"

"I'm Acting U.S. Marshal Pete Nash," the lead rider said. "I have a warrant for the arrest of Carsten McNeil for the murder of U.S. Marshal Ross Cooper. Shot him in the back."

Morris froze. He fell silent as a tapping sound came from behind him. "Why would he do a thing like that?" Morris said. "My brother would never kill nobody who wasn't tryin' to kill him first."

"Do you have the warrant?" Vince asked as he hobbled outside on his crutch, sitting down in his favorite chair on the porch.

Nash dismounted and hitched his horse on the porch rail. He produced a folded-up warrant from his pocket and handed it over. Vince skimmed it over. Tears welled in his eyes.

"Your son is a viper," Nash said. "He deceived us all. He was soft on the criminals we arrested and now has broken a wanted felon out of custody. We need to search your property. If he's here, you'll be arrested for aiding and abetting a wanted felon, and you'll face eternal damnation." He gestured for the other riders to dismount.

Two of them drew guns and entered the barn. Another approached them.

"My brother ain't a felon," Morris said, tightening his grip on the rifle. "And you'd best watch what you're sayin'."

"Morris!" Vince snapped. "Let 'em search the place. We've got nothing to hide, but I'll be sending them a bill if they break anything."

Nash and the deputy walked past them into the house. As the sound of furniture being moved echoed from within, Morris turned to McElroy and the other rider, a Mexican woman. She glared at him. He walked over to them.

"That's far enough, hombre," she said, drawing a revolver and training it on him.

"You friends with that rip?" Morris said to her, nodding toward McElroy.

"He just showed us where you lived," she replied. "He ain't deputized. I'm gonna shoot him if he tries anything."

"Good," Morris said. "That'll save me the job."

"Vasquez!" Nash called to her as he left the house. "We do not pay you to make friends with a criminal's allies."

"I'm not being paid at all," she replied. "I'm paid when I bring folks in."

The other two deputies left the barn. They looked toward Nash and shook their heads.

"I told you my brother ain't here," he said to the marshal. "Now you'd best ride on."

"Don't give us a reason to come back," Nash said. "You're not without sin just yet."

"Never said I was," Morris said as the posse mounted their horses and trotted out of the yard.

***

The family said nothing as they gathered around the dinner table. The bean casserole sat cooling on their plates.

"Something ain't right," Morris said. "I can't see Carsten shootin' Marshal Cooper in the back. Especially since McElroy seemed to be ridin' with the posse."

"McElroy was with them?" Attie said, thumping the table. "Why the hell was he ridin' with the marshals?"

"Attie, you're not helping!" Cassie snapped.

Vince rested his hand on her arm, soothing her.

"McElroy's wanted for breakin' out of Yuma," Morris continued. "And there's somethin' off 'bout that Nash fella. I reckon I gotta look into this."

"What do you mean?" Vince said. "The warrant was real."

"That don't mean the charges are," Morris said as he stood up. "I want to find out what Carsten got in trouble for. I'm headin' to Phoenix."

"I'm comin' too," Attie said. "He did the same for me."

"All right," Morris said, "but you gotta keep your head. You can't go shootin' at McElroy as soon as you lay eyes on him."

"What do you hope to prove?" Vince said. "If Carsten has killed a marshal and broken someone out of jail, he's going to be hunted by every lawman in the territory. If you're asking around, you might be arrested too. How can you prove innocence for things like that?"

"It's a risk that'll need takin'," Morris said.

"Mr. McNeil," Davey said, raising his hand, "I reckon Morris is right. I don't wanna go speakin' ill of Carsten unless

I knew he's done those things. I reckon we should head to Phoenix and ask around."

"No," Morris said. "I'm gonna need you and Mike to tend the ranch. You're part owners, after all. Leave this to Attie and me."

Davey sat down and pouted.

"Don't worry," Morris added. "She'll be fine. We'll leave for Prescott in the morning and take the next train to Phoenix." He placed a hand on Vince's shoulder.

"We'll be fine," Attie said. "We'll prove Carsten's innocent."

Vince and Cassie looked at Morris with blank expressions.

"Be careful," Davey said. "And don't get Attie into trouble."

***

The following day, Morris rode into Prescott with Attie as the sun was coming up. Morris looked over his shoulders, seeing if any riders were following them. He hitched Blondie outside the station. As he waited in line for the ticket office, he noticed a sheriff's deputy hammering a wanted poster to the nearby noticeboard. Carsten's face stared out from the poster.

"Mornin'," the deputy said as he noticed Morris looking at the poster. "I've got some spares if you want to take one of those."

"Nah," Morris said as he stroked his chin. "I ain't a bounty hunter."

"It's a real shame," the deputy said. "Carsten was a good kid and a great lawman. I don't know what drove him to kill his boss. Sheriff Horne's beside himself. He was a good friend of Carsten, and he's gotta arrest him if'n he comes back."

"Well, maybe there was some devil in him," Morris said, not wanting to reveal his connection. He turned away from the deputy as he and Attie stepped up to the window.

"Mornin', folks," the clerk said. "How can I help you?"

"Two tickets to Phoenix, please." Morris said. "And space for two horses in the livery car."

"That'll be twelve dollars," the clerk replied.

Morris cursed under his breath as he dug into his pocket for the money and handed it over. After collecting the tickets, Morris sat on the bench on the platform beside Attie. "Everyone 'round here will be thinkin' he did it," he said as he stared at the railroad tracks in the distance.

"We'll prove his innocence," Attie said. "Then what will people say?"

"I don't know," Morris said. "Maybe some will believe it, maybe some won't. Maybe we're wrong." He heard a train whistle in the distance. "I guess that says only time will tell," he added as he stood up.

***

It was noon by the time the train rolled into Phoenix. Morris wiped the sweat from his brow as he heaved himself out of the wooden seat. Through the steam, he noticed several men with guns waiting on the platform. He nudged Attie.

"What is it?" she said, "We here?"

"Yup," Morris said, "and it looks like we got ourselves a welcomin' committee."

As the train lurched to a halt, a man in a gray suit and bowler hat stepped into Morris and Attie's passenger car, carrying a walking stick. Morris noticed a sheriff's badge on his lapel. He turned around. Another man entered at the opposite end of the passenger car, standing in the doorway.

"Ladies and gentlemen," the man in the suit said, "I'm Maricopa County Sheriff John Garrett. Sorry for the delay in travel plans, but I believe there are two passengers on this train who are accomplices of Carsten McNeil. I received a telegram saying they boarded at Prescott."

Morris grabbed Attie's wrist as the man looked in their direction.

"What do we do?" she hissed. "Someone must have followed us or turned nose."

"We surrender," Morris replied in a low tone. "We're corralled, and I ain't gonna start a gunfight that's likely to hurt a couple of bystanders." He stood up and raised his hands, gesturing for Attie to do the same. "Looks like you caught us," he said as he approached the sheriff, removing his gun belt. "Perhaps you'd care to explain the charges against us?"

"Accessory to the murder of U.S. Marshal Ross Cooper," Garrett replied. "Now, off this train."

Morris and Attie stepped onto the platform, where the sheriff's deputies kept revolvers or shotguns trained on them.

"Can we go to the livery car?" he asked. "We brought our horses with us."

"Make sure we get their horses." Garrett turned to his deputies. "We'll charge them for the stabling."

"You know we can hear you?" Attie said.

"Yeah," Morris added, "and I ain't movin' an inch till you tell me what we're bein' charged with. How are we accessories? I ain't even been to Phoenix before."

"I've got some comfortable cells for you down at my office," Garrett said. "We'll talk there."

***

Morris held his breath as he approached the cell.

"Get in there!" the deputy said, shoving him inside.

The barred door was slammed behind Morris, followed by a scrape of wood. He turned around and saw Garrett dragging a chair into the holding area.

"Now that you're comfortable," he said, "perhaps you can enlighten me about what you're doing here. And I don't like liars. They're just as bad as people trying to escape and will be dealt with the same way." He produced a revolver from his holster and cocked it.

"Fine," Morris said as he sat down on the cot in the cell. "I'm Morris McNeil, and that's my sister, Attie."

"You're connected to Carsten McNeil?" Garrett asked.

"He's our brother," Morris said. "We got visited by some marshal called Nash. Said Carsten had killed Marshal Cooper, so we asked around here. Did anyone even see the killin'?"

"Someone shot Marshal Cooper in the back while leaving a saloon," Garrett said. "We found your brother's gun at the scene. There aren't many people out here who still use a cap and ball Remington."

"Maybe someone took it," Attie said. "Tried to frame him."

Garrett stared at her before looking back at Morris. "Your sister has a vivid imagination," he said. "But I don't have the time or inclination to indulge it. As soon as I recovered the gun, I went to Carsten's hotel room to arrest him. But he fled with his gal."

"Fleur's with him?" Attie said.

"Will you be quiet, please?" Garrett snapped. "At this moment, I'm talking to your brother."

"You talk to me," Morris said, as he stood up and pressed against the bars, "and you talk to my sister at the same time. What happened next?"

"He sprung a known stagecoach robber named Wiley Frye out of prison," Garrett continued. "Then broke into the livery to steal horses, assaulting the owner. Yes, your brother's certainly an upstanding citizen."

Morris closed his eyes and rested his head on the bars.

"So what's gonna happen to us?" Attie said.

"You'll be tried as his accomplices," Garrett replied. "Unless you can think of a reason not to be."

***

As night fell, Morris lay on the cot and stared at the ceiling. He heard footsteps; someone entering the building.

"Marshal Nash," Garrett said, "I detained Carsten's siblings after receiving your telegram. Just give the word and I'll have them in your custody."

"Have they said anything about Carsten?" Nash asked. "They don't matter to me. All that matters is laying a righteous punishment on him."

"Well, he isn't in this county," Garrett said. "Maybe he's heading for the border. We could head him off at the pass at

Tucson. It'll take at least four days for him to get there, but only two days on the train. But that's another county. If you're willing to deputize me, I'll be able to go with them."

"Agreed," Nash replied.

Morris perked up as he listened to them. "Why is a sheriff so interested in goin' after him?" he mumbled to himself.

"Psst..." Attie said.

Morris looked up. "What do you want?" he replied.

"I've got an idea," she said. "Just follow my lead." Attie rattled the door to her cell. "Take us with you!" she called.

The conversation in the other room halted. Nash and Garrett entered the holding area.

"Why should we take you with us?" Garrett asked.

"You want Carsten real bad, right?" Attie replied.

"He murdered a man he was subordinate to in cold blood," Nash said. "I will ensure he faces damnation for his sin."

"I'll take that as a yes," Attie said as she took a step back from Nash. "But if'n you're goin' after him, why not take us with you? We could convince him to give himself up."

Morris gaped. Nash and Garrett exchanged a glance. Attie gave him a wink, and he raised his brow.

"Very well," Nash said. "You can atone for your brother's sins by ensuring we bring him to justice."

Morris gave Attie a look of repulsion.

Chapter 18
From Dusk Till Don's

Carsten rubbed his chin as he and his companions reached the outskirts of Tucson. His legs ached, and he struggled to keep his eyes open as the midday sun bore down on them.

"You're almost looking like Morris with that beard," Fleur said with a weak chuckle.

"You think it suits me?" he replied. "I can't imagine myself with a soup catcher."

"No," Fleur said, "me neither."

"So, what kind of place does your cousin run?" Carsten asked Wiley.

"Just a quaint little cantina with everythin' a fella could need," Wiley replied. "Food, liquor, cards, and plenty of soiled doves for a good time. That's if you have the energy after four days of ridin'."

"I don't think Miss Fleur would approve," Carsten said. "Right now, I could use a night in a proper bed."

"This way," Wiley said. "It's off the trail over yonder. But you'll need to do somethin' 'bout that." He pulled the marshal's badge off Carsten's jacket and threw it away.

"Hey!" Carsten said.

"No lawmen here," Wiley replied. "Rock up wearin' that badge and you'll be filled with more holes than a colander."

Carsten followed Wiley's route. The trio reached an abode two-story building surrounded by a curtain wall with a wooden gate. A sign by the gate said From Dusk Till Don's Inn and Stables. Lively guitar music came from behind the wall.

Wiley dismounted and knocked on the gates. Someone aimed a shotgun at him through an embrasure in the gate. "Open up!" Wiley called. "It's Wiley and two guests!"

The shotgun was withdrawn. The gates opened to reveal a courtyard. Three men sat around a cooking fire, drinking and laughing, while one of them strummed a guitar. Their chatter and music stopped as Carsten walked his horse inside. He and Fleur dismounted, handing their reins to a stable hand while Carsten kept his view of the three men.

"Come on," Wiley said. "Let's meet Don."

Carsten nodded in agreement, then one man from the fire stood in front of him.

"I know who you are," he said. "The law don't fly 'round here, Quaker McNeil." He patted the Peacemaker in his holster.

Carsten moved to walk around, but the man sidestepped and blocked his path.

"Reach for it," he growled.

Carsten grabbed the revolver from the bully's holster and struck him across the face with it.

He reeled back. The other two men stood up.

Carsten tossed the gun into his other hand and drew his Colt. "Go ahead," he told them. "Make your move."

"Hey!" a voice called from inside the house. "No gunfightin' in my place!"

The bully's two friends let go of their guns and directed their friend to sit down. Carsten holstered his Colt but kept hold of the Peacemaker.

A man in a well-worn suit approached the newcomers. "Well, I'll be," he said as he embraced Wiley. "It's good to see you again, cousin."

"Don," Wiley replied, "these here are my friends, Carsten McNeil and the lovely Miss Fleur. They sprung me outta the hoosegow and need a place to lie low."

Don looked Carsten over. "Any friend of Wiley's is a friend of mine," he said. "Even if'n they are lawmen."

"I'm as good as fired anyhow," Carsten replied.

"Why don't you come on in?" Don said. "You folks look like you could use a meal and a splash of whiskey."

Carsten followed Don into the cantina. Four rugged-looking figures played poker, while three women in threadbare dresses loitered by the bar. Don gestured for them to sit at the table in an alcove in the corner. Carsten sat with his back to the wall.

Don approached the table with a bottle of whiskey and four glasses. "So, what brings you folks to my place anyhow?" he asked as he poured the whiskey.

"We're lookin' for el Presidente," Carsten said before Wiley could reply. He noticed the card players turned to face him.

"Your buddy's still a lawman at heart," Don said to Wiley. "And he's in way over his head. Fact of the matter is you don't find el Presidente. He finds you. You've got one night to stay here, then you'll need to be on your way."

Wiley bowed his head.

"You folks want some grub?" Don asked. "My cook makes a mean chili."

"Sure," Carsten said. "Some grub would be good."

As Don left the table, Wiley punched Carsten in the arm. "What the hell were you thinkin'?" he said as he glowered at him. "Most of these folks are outlaws, and most of them are scared of el Presidente. You coulda gotten us killed. I don't know any other place we can hide out." He knocked back the whiskey like it was water.

***

An hour later, Carsten sat and stared at the empty bowl on the table. The card circle had kept playing, periodically visited by one of the saloon girls to refill their drinks.

"Carsten," Fleur said, "if we can't stay here, where can we go?"

"I'm stumped," Carsten said. "We gotta find out who el Presidente is and prove he killed Marshal Cooper. I ain't cut out for life on the run."

Don, standing behind the bar, nodded to the card players as they were served. He polished two glasses and ducked behind the bar. A scraping of chairs prompted Carsten to reach for his Colt.

"I wouldn't do that if I was you," Don said, pointing a shotgun at them.

The card players were aiming their revolvers at Carsten and his companions. He stood up and raised his hands.

"Don?" Wiley asked as he raised his hands. "What are you doin'?"

"El Presidente's in Phoenix," Don replied. "He arrived the day before you did and told me you might be comin'. He told me to hold you here till he arrived."

"You backstabbin' son of a trug!" Wiley yelled.

"It's up to you," Don said. "The lawman he wants alive to make an example of. He don't much care for the rest of you. Take them upstairs."

The card players advanced. Carsten stepped into the open and kept his hands raised as two of the men approached him and Wiley. He looked around. Don kept his shotgun trained on them from his position behind the bar.

One of the card players leered at Fleur as he grabbed her arm and pulled her from the alcove. She grabbed the whiskey bottle on the table and smashed it in his face. He screamed, covering his eyes. Wiley surged forward and tackled him.

Carsten punched the man closest to him, drew his Colt, and fired at the bar. Whiskey bottles smashed, spilling their contents behind the bar. Don took cover.

Carsten dived behind another table and flipped it over. Shots rang out. Smoke filled the room. He felt splinters fly from the table as the men fired at him. He emerged and fired a shot.

One of the card players dropped.

Carsten glimpsed Wiley and Fleur in the alcove.

Wiley nodded to him as he shot the fourth outlaw. "Don!" Wiley yelled as he lit a stogie. "If you value this place, you'd best come out. Or else I'm gonna burn this place down."

"Okay," Don replied. The shotgun flew out from behind the bar. Don emerged with his hands raised.

Carsten stood up and advanced, keeping his gun trained on him. "You're gonna tell me what I want to know," Carsten said. "If el Presidente's comin' what does he look like?"

"Fine," Don said. "I'm probably gonna die anyhow. I don't know what he looks like. Some tinhorn showed up claimin' to have a letter from el Presidente. But he's comin' by tonight."

"What did this tinhorn look like?" Carsten said.

"Fancy riding duds," Don replied. "Had a distinct moustache. Sounded real slimy."

"Garrett…" Carsten mumbled.

"Yeah, that was the guy!" Don cried out as he heard the name. "His handle was Garrett."

"He's another lawman," Carsten said. "How come he wasn't shot on sight?"

"Dude never struck me as a lawman," Don replied. "But he's been here before. Shot a fella for talkin' back, then said he was a messenger for el Presidente. As soon as everyone found out he worked for el Presidente, nobody wanted to mess with him."

"Well, it'll be interestin' for you to know that he's the sheriff of Maricopa County," Wiley said. "But if he ain't el Presidente, I wonder who is?"

"Hell if I know," Don replied. "Like I said, I've only known el Presidente to contact via letters and dead drops."

"If'n he's comin'," Carsten said, "then we'd best get ready. I'm gonna check on the three outside." He stepped into the courtyard.

The three men by the cooking fire stood up as they saw him and fled into the stables.

Chapter 19
Revelation

Carsten looked at his watch as he sat by the door to the cantina. He rested his Colt Frontier on his lap. Wiley sat in a chair in the center of the room with his hands behind his back. Fleur stood behind the bar with Don. She had exchanged her dress for that of one of the saloon girls. She aimed a disdainful glare at Wiley as she rested a hand on Don's shoulder while pressing a derringer into his side.

"What's with the evil eye from you, sweetheart?" Wiley asked.

"This dress is uncomfortable," Fleur replied.

"You gotta look the part 'round here," Wiley replied. "Now keep quiet. Carsten's supposed to be dead, and I'm a prisoner."

There was a knock at the door.

"Who is it?" Don called out.

"I have a message from el Presidente," Garrett's voice replied.

Don nodded to Carsten. He stood up and pulled the door open, ensuring he remained behind it and out of sight. Garrett stepped inside. He'd exchanged his gray suit for trail clothes.

"Howdy, sheriff," Wiley said with a grin. "Bet you didn't tell my cousin 'bout your day job."

"I don't have time for games," Garrett replied. "Don, where's Carsten? That's his sweetheart resting on your shoulder."

"Right here," Carsten said. He slammed the door and cocked his revolver, aiming it at the sheriff. "A little out of your jurisdiction, ain't ya?"

Wiley stood up and revealed the two revolvers he'd hidden behind the chair. He winked at the sheriff as he trained the guns on him.

Carsten bolted the door and removed the gun from Garrett's holster, tossing it aside. "Since you're here," Carsten said, "you can tell me who this Presidente fella is."

"You still believe that story?" Garrett said.

"A lot more than I did," Carsten replied. "Why don't you sit down? You keep your hands flat on that tabletop, and we'll talk 'bout how you're gonna get me outta this hole you threw me in." He gestured with his gun to a table by the bar.

Garrett sat down.

Carsten sat opposite, keeping his gun pointed at him.

"You'll hang for this," Garrett said. "I brought a posse with me."

"I doubt that," Carsten said. "This ain't Maricopa County."

"Are you expecting me to explain some scheme?" Garrett said.

"I was gonna try to explain it myself," Carsten replied. "I ain't cut out for life outside the law, but I had a couple thoughts this past week 'bout the journey. When you sent me after Wiley Frye, I figured it was 'cause you couldn't go after him yourself since he was in the next county. When he talked 'bout el Presidente, I figured it was some kinda tall yarn. But when you sent Dixie Jack to dry gulch us, I started suspectin' somethin' wasn't right."

"This story's getting better by the moment," Garrett said with a grin.

"Well," he continued, "I reckon it ain't a coincidence you tried to send me to the hoosegow for my gunfight with Fast Eddie after I mentioned el Presidente to you. You became almost as fanatical as Nash in layin' down the law, so clearly you reckoned I knew something I wasn't supposed to. And then you had someone break into my hotel and steal my shootin' iron so you could kill the marshal and frame me for it."

"Again," Garrett said, "you have no evidence."

"Oh, but I do," Carsten replied. "After I broke Wiley outta the hoosegow, which I reckon I'll have sacrificed my career as a lawman to do, he led me to this place. And it seems his cousin over there knows you're a regular. Now, here you are. Don can be a witness."

"You finished?" the sheriff said. "I'd clap, but you asked me to keep my hands on the table. Anyway, it's still your word against mine."

The sound of banging on the door prompted Carsten to leap out of his chair. He noticed Garrett looked toward the door with a look of concern.

"Carsten McNeil!" Nash's voice barked. "Throw down your guns and come out with your hands up! You've got nowhere left to run!"

"You ain't bluffin' 'bout the posse?" Wiley said.

"I never said it was a county posse," Garrett replied. "I've been deputized by Acting Marshal Nash, and I've already arrested two of your accomplices."

"What accomplices?" Carsten said. "I don't have no accomplices except for the ones in this room right now."

"Give yourself up, please!" another voice shouted.

Carsten felt a lump in his throat as he recognized his brother's voice. "Morris?" he called as he pressed against the window. "What are you doin' here?"

"Me and Attie came to find you when we heard 'bout the warrant," Morris replied. "The sheriff nabbed us, then Attie convinced 'em to take us with 'em. Convince you to surrender."

"Seemed like a good idea at the time!" Attie said.

"I'll bet..." Carsten said to himself.

"Carsten!" Nash said. "If you don't listen to your siblings, we'll smoke you out!"

"I've got the sheriff in here!" Carsten replied. "And I reckon he's got some explainin' to do! Somethin' tells me he came out here on his lonesome. And I've got a witness who'll testify to his corruption."

"This is your last chance!" Nash said. "You need to answer for your sins!"

A shot rang out behind Carsten. A scream followed. He turned around. Don and Fleur had disappeared behind the bar. He glimpsed the derringer in Garrett's hand. The sheriff flipped the table. Carsten raised his Colt.

"Look out!" Wiley shouted.

Carsten dived to the ground as he heard shots outside. A barrage of gunfire raked the cantina. He felt splinters from the shutters land on him. He looked up at the door. The lock exploded, and the door flew open.

Nash emerged carrying a shotgun, followed by Ramona. Nash trained his gun on Carsten while Ramona aimed at Wiley, who threw down his revolvers.

"Fleur?" Carsten called out toward the bar.

"I'm fine!" she replied. "Don's hit, though. He's bleeding pretty badly."

"He was pulling a gun," Garrett said. "Thankfully, I still had a derringer and shot him."

"Damn it…" Carsten said under his breath.

Nash replied with a kick to his stomach. "That's for old times," he said. "Now everyone, outside!"

After being disarmed and handcuffed, Carsten found himself herded out into the courtyard with Wiley and Fleur. He noticed Morris and Attie in a prison wagon. McElroy stood guarding them alongside Charlie and Ike.

"You folks just get in the wagon," Garrett said.

"What about Don?" Carsten said.

"The Lord has delivered," Nash said as he stepped outside. "I imagined you would hide in this den of iniquity."

"That's my cousin you're talkin' 'bout," Wiley growled at Nash.

"Silence!" Nash replied.

"If you could stop preachin' fire and brimstone for five minutes," Carsten said, "you might want to hear this."

"Hear what?" Nash said.

"Haven't you asked yourself why the sheriff is ridin' with you?" Carsten said. "He didn't ride with us on the trail of

Wiley Frye initially. So why's he ridin' now? And what's he doin' way out here?"

"He wanted to ride out alone on an errand," Morris said. "Somethin' 'bout that don't sit well."

"Sí," Ramona said, nodding in agreement.

"You might as well confess," Carsten said. "I know you're involved with el Presidente. Who is he?" He smiled as he noticed the posse members glare at Garrett, who fidgeted.

"It's him!" McElroy shouted, pointing at the sheriff. "He's el Presidente! I recognize the voice from when he paid me to steal Carsten's gun!"

"You yellow bastard!" Garrett snarled. He drew his revolver and shot McElroy, diving into the stables. "Now, boys!"

Several gunfighters emerged from the stables and opened fire. Carsten pressed to the ground. Nash fell, clutching his bloodied chest. Carsten grabbed the revolver from his holster and ran toward the prison wagon. Morris and Attie had pressed to the wooden floor as bullets flew through the cage. Carsten shot the lock off the cage door and yanked it open.

"Get inside!" Ramona shouted above the gunshots. She returned fire with her Winchester as Fleur scuttled into the cantina. The outlaws took cover in the stables.

Carsten fired toward the stables as Morris and Attie ran to the cantina.

"Come on!" Morris yelled.

Carsten ran after him and dived through the doorway. Ramona slammed the door closed and pressed against it.

"What about Charlie and Ike?" Carsten asked.

"Muertos," Ramona said through clenched teeth.

Carsten noticed blood seeping through a wound on her leg and another in her side. "You're hit!"

"They're clean," she replied. "Went straight through."

"We gotta patch you up!" Fleur said.

"We ain't goin' nowhere," Wiley remarked, skimming his handcuffs across the floor and holding up a lock pick with glee.

Carsten smiled as the sounds of gunfire died down.

"Looks like you're trapped!" Garrett's voice called out. "Lawmen should know better than trying to raid From Dusk Till Don's. May he rest in peace."

"Then you'd best watch your back!" Carsten replied as Wiley picked the lock on his handcuffs. He noticed the discarded guns and gun belts on the table.

"Yeah," Ramona added, "I recognized Floyd Whitfield out there. The Blacksnake Gang ain't fond of lawmen."

"They know I'm el Presidente," Garrett replied.

"Thanks for confirming that," Carsten said as he put on his gun belt and loaded his Colt Frontier.

"Well, you're not in a position to tell anyone," Garrett said.

Carsten peered through a bullet hole in the door. He saw one outlaw approaching with a can. "Blazes," he said. "They're gonna burn us out."

A shot rang out. He looked through the bullet hole. The outlaw lay dead. Attie crouched beneath the window, blowing smoke from her revolver.

Carsten nodded to her. More shots came from outside. "Well," he said, "we might as well die together."

Ramona nodded and cocked her Winchester. She lay prone in front of the doorway. Carsten swung the door open. She fired several shots before rolling behind the wall. Carsten emerged, firing at another outlaw. The man dropped. The shots outside died down.

Carsten noticed the prison wagon leaving through the gates. "He's lightin' out!"

Ramona fired a shot. It impacted in the wall.

"I need him alive!" Carsten yelled, as he pushed down the rifle. "He needs to stand trial!" He ran outside, followed by Morris and Attie.

They ran toward the stables. The gunfire had died down, but it still smelled like powder smoke.

Carsten aimed his revolver and entered the stable. An outlaw emerged from the stall, clutching his torso. Carsten ducked behind the door. A pistol cracked. Splinters flew from the door. Carsten sprang from cover and returned fire. The outlaw dropped. Carsten took a breath as he noticed the saddles on a bench in the corner. He grabbed one and threw it over Dan's back.

Wiley ran inside after him, along with Morris and Attie.

"We heard a shot," Morris said.

"It's clear," Carsten said. "I'm goin' after Garrett 'fore he gets away."

"What happens if he gets away?" Morris asked.

"I can't clear my name," Carsten replied as he cinched the saddle. "We have to get him."

"There's a mountain path," Wiley said. "It's too big for that wagon, but we could use it to head 'em off."

"We?" Carsten said.

"You ain't thinkin' of goin' after him alone?" Wiley said with a grin as he saddled another horse. "This ain't somethin' you have to do yourself. I got an ax to grind with him, too."

"Me too!" Morris said. "The McNeils don't cower to nobody, and we protect each other."

"Your family certainly is determined," Ramona said.

Carsten turned around. The bounty hunter lumbered into the stable with her rifle, struggling to stand. Fleur entered behind her, trying to keep her standing.

"It's gonna be a rough ride," Carsten said. "Think you'll manage it?"

"She's not fit to ride," Fleur said. "I'm gonna stay here and try to patch her up, but she's gonna need a doctor."

"Maybe I should ride into town," Morris said. "Me and Attie can get a doctor and perhaps some reinforcements."

"That ain't a good idea," Wiley said as he mounted his horse.

"We gotta bring him in," Carsten replied.

"Carsten..." Fleur said.

He turned around. "What is it?" he asked as he saw tears welling in her eyes.

"Be careful," she said, kissing him.

He held his arms around her. "I'll be back," he said as he mounted Dan. "I promise."

"Let's ride!" Wiley said, lashing his reins and loping out of the stable.

***

The sun was setting as Carsten and Wiley rode across the mountain path. Below, Carsten saw the prison wagon rolling along the wider trail. Garrett and Whitfield sat in the driver's seat.

"There they are," Wiley said. "Let's get 'em." He rode at full gallop down the path that connected to the main trail.

Carsten spurred Dan on, aiming himself behind the wagon. "Remember, I want Garrett alive." He pulled up his bandana after he inhaled some trail dust kicked up by the wheels and team.

Whitfield looked behind him and saw the two approaching. He raised a revolver and fired at them. Carsten felt the bullet fly past him. He spurred Dan on while returning fire with his Colt. His shots went wide, as the bobbing of the horse threw off his aim. Another shot rang out behind Carsten. Whitfield tumbled off the wagon with a sharp scream.

Carsten looked behind him.

"You're all clear!" Wiley called. "Get the bastard!"

Carsten nodded. He brought Dan beside the wagon and leaped out of the saddle. He grabbed the cage as his legs dragged along the ground. He gritted his teeth and lifted them, resting on the wagon's suspension. He moved his hands up the cage, trying to find a foothold.

Garrett turned and saw him on the side of the wagon. He pulled one of the reins. The horses whinnied as they turned. The wagon lurched sideways.

Carsten tightened his grip on the cage. He clenched his teeth as the metal dug into his hands. He heaved himself up to the top of the wagon.

Garrett looked behind again. Carsten slid into the seat and grappled the sheriff. The two exchanged punches as the wagon raced off the trail, causing it to rumble more violently. Garrett's eyes widened as he saw they were approaching a cliff.

"I'll never go to jail!" Garrett snarled. "You'll never charge me!"

Carsten responded with a punch to the jaw. Garrett slumped back. Carsten grabbed the reins and yanked them forward. The wagon lurched as it hit a rock, taking off one of the wheels. He grabbed Garrett and threw himself off as the team came loose and galloped away.

The pair rolled across the rocky ground. Carsten grabbed Garrett's arm as he rolled off the edge of the cliff. He winced as he saw the prison wagon smash to pieces at the bottom.

"No!" Garrett screamed as he looked down. "Don't let it end like this!"

Carsten tried to move, but Garrett weighed him down. He heard a crumbling sound beneath him. "Give me your other hand!" he said to the sheriff.

Garrett said nothing. He looked at Carsten and back down toward the drop. A smile came to his lips. "You know," he said, "if I die today, the truth dies with me."

"Don't even think about it," Carsten said as he heard the clatter of hooves behind him.

Wiley appeared beside Carsten and reached for Garrett's shoulder. "Come on!" he said. "Pull!"

Carsten heaved, wincing at his bumps and bruises from the fall. They pulled Garrett up. The sheriff moved to jump. Wiley floored him with a punch. Carsten gave a thankful nod to Wiley as he hauled Garrett to his feet.

"So what happens now?" Wiley asked.

"I guess we're even," Carsten said. "I've saved your life, and you've saved mine. The law will probably still pursue you, but I'll give you a head start. I've got who I came for."

Wiley nodded and shook Carsten's hand. Carsten watched him mount his horse and ride away, eventually disappearing over the horizon.

The stars shone as Carsten led Garrett and Dan back to the cantina. He glimpsed firelight through the gates and then could see Morris and Attie sitting by the fire. They looked up as they saw him.

"He's back!" Morris shouted in excitement.

Carsten dropped Garrett in front of him. He winced as his siblings and Fleur embraced him. Ramona sat on a box by the fire with bandages around her leg and torso. She gave Carsten a proud smile. He looked around and saw several armed men with tin stars surrounding him.

"You must be Quaker McNeil," one of them said. "I'm the marshal of Tucson, and your brother has told me quite a story."

"It's one I need to tell the judge," Carsten replied. "I think Sheriff Garrett here owes us a mighty explanation."

"Well," the marshal said, "you do too. There's a warrant for your arrest, and I gotta take you in."

Carsten nodded and smiled, holding his hands out in front of him. "Well," he said, "I reckon this time I gotta let you take me in. After all, Miss Vasquez needs to earn her keep."

Chapter 20
All Sins Forgiven

A week later, Carsten sat in the courtroom in Phoenix. Ambrose Cunningham sat beside him, looking over a large bundle of notes. The handcuffs chafed Carsten's wrists, and he avoided making eye contact with the two deputy marshals who stood behind him.

Sheriff Garrett and Reed Kirkham sat at the opposite table. Garrett was also handcuffed and flanked by deputies. Carsten listened to the murmurs of the jurors and the townspeople in the gallery.

"All rise for Judge Moses Day!" the bailiff called once again.

The black-clad judge sat down at his bench and banged his gavel. "Court is now in session," he said. "I will hear the case of Carsten McNeil versus Sheriff John Garrett. I understand Carsten McNeil is being charged with the murder of U.S. Marshal Ross Cooper and aiding and abetting the escape of Wiley Frye. Carsten McNeil, how do you plead?"

"Not guilty on the charge of murder, your honor," Carsten replied. "And guilty on the charge of aiding and abetting."

"Very well," the judge said. "In the meantime, I also understand Sheriff John Garrett is simultaneously being charged with extortion, corruption, and the murder of Glen McElroy and that these court cases are intertwined. John Garrett, how do you plead?"

"Not guilty on all counts, your honor," Garrett replied.

"Would the clerk of the court please note for the record the pleas of McNeil and Garrett?" the judge said. "Then we shall proceed. Would Carsten McNeil approach the bench?"

Carsten stood up, escorted by one deputy. The bailiff held out a Bible. Carsten placed his hand on it.

"Do you solemnly swear to tell the truth, the whole truth, and nothing but the truth, so help me, God?" the bailiff asked.

"I do," Carsten replied before sitting in the witness chair.

Ambrose stepped forward. "Carsten McNeil, can you explain the past two weeks to the jury?" he asked.

"I was part of a federal posse under Ross Cooper," Carsten began. "They had sent us to apprehend Wiley Frye at the behest of Sheriff Garrett."

"Objection!" Kirkham shouted. "Relevance."

"I'm trying to establish where the knowledge of the individual known as el Presidente came from, your honor," Ambrose replied.

"Objection overruled," the judge said. "Proceed, Mr. Cunningham."

"Were you aware of the reasons behind Sheriff Garrett's instructions?" Ambrose continued.

"It didn't seem too suspicious at the time," Carsten said. "He was aware Wiley's hideout was in Pinal County, where he had no authority. We apprehended Wiley Frye, during which time he spoke of an individual known as el Presidente. During the journey, a sharpshooter bushwhacked us. He seemed to target Wiley Frye."

"Objection!" Kirkham shouted. "Speculative."

"Sustained," the judge said.

"During the ambush, they killed another deputy," Carsten said. "I was taking cover beside Wiley until I could close the distance and corner the shooter. He spoke of Wiley Frye being a traitor, but I was forced to shoot him in self-defense 'fore I could get anythin' else outta him."

"Were you able to identify the man who ambushed you?" Ambrose asked.

"Marshal Cooper identified him as a former Confederate sharpshooter named Corporal Jack Dixon, also known as Dixie Jack," Carsten answered. "Upon our return to Phoenix, I discussed the matter of el Presidente with Sheriff Garrett."

***

The afternoon sun cast shadows through the blinds in the courtroom. Carsten had sat through testimonies from his siblings and Fleur, along with Ramona and the marshal who had been guarding Wiley Frye.

"As you can see, your honor," Ambrose summed up, "they framed my client for the murder of Marshal Ross Cooper by the late Mr. McElroy at the behest of Sheriff Garrett, under the persona of el Presidente. McElroy, whom I may remind the jury had escaped from Yuma Territorial Prison four weeks earlier, was killed by Mr. Garrett when he confessed to Marshal Cooper's murder, according to the testimony of the witnesses present.

"After a search of Sheriff Garrett's residence, we discovered ledgers in a hidden room detailing payoffs made by outlaw gangs, including Wiley Frye's. The murder of Marshal Cooper and subsequent framing of Deputy McNeil were part of an elaborate plan to prevent either of them from discovering this conspiracy.

"Although my client has pleaded guilty to aiding and abetting the escape of Wiley Frye, I may argue that his actions were necessary in discovering the conspiracy. My defense rests."

"Thank you, Mr. Cunningham," the judge said. "Mr. Kirkham, if you please."

"Thank you, your honor," Kirkham said, approaching the bench.

***

Carsten fidgeted, waiting for the proceedings to conclude. Kirkham had interviewed the livery owner, whom Wiley had struck down. He still regretted that action.

"Mister foreman," the judge said, "what is your verdict on John Garrett?"

Carsten felt his heart thumping.

"Your honor," the jury foreman replied, "we find Mr. Garrett guilty on all counts."

"And your verdict on Carsten McNeil?"

"Not guilty, your honor."

Ambrose patted Carsten on the shoulder.

The judge faced Garrett. "John Garrett," he said with a stern tone, "this court finds you guilty of corruption, unlawful imprisonment, extortion, and the murders of Glen McElroy and U.S. Marshal Ross Cooper. You have clearly been abusing your position to get information about the security of stagecoaches and trains traveling in this county and selling it to those who sought to rob them. We hereby sentence you to hang by the neck until you are dead. May God have mercy on your soul." He banged his gavel.

The two deputies escorted the former sheriff out of the courtroom.

The judge turned to Carsten, who held his breath. "Carsten McNeil," he said, "you assaulted a fellow deputy marshal, dynamited a building, and aided and abetted in the escape of a wanted felon who remains at large. However, you also went above and beyond the call of duty in solving a murder which you were initially accused of and uncovering a conspiracy that could have undermined this whole territory. Although you have pleaded guilty to these charges, I believe your actions were necessary to uncover the conspiracy. In gratitude, the charges rallied against you are being dropped, and we will wipe your criminal record clean. Congratulations." He banged his gavel again.

Applause followed from the onlookers. One marshal removed Carsten's handcuffs who rubbed his wrists and turned to embrace Fleur and his siblings.

"This court is adjourned."

Carsten left the courtroom holding Fleur's hand. Journalists swarmed him, bombarding him with questions.

"Mr. McNeil, will you consider the marshal's position?" one asked.

"Mr. McNeil, have you been reinstated to your post?" another asked.

"Mr. McNeil, what are your thoughts on the sheriff's conviction?" a third asked.

Carsten said nothing, raising his hand for silence. As he stared, the three journalists backed away.

"I'll just put a 'no comment' on that one," the first journalist said.

"The fanfare for bein' a hero ain't great," Morris remarked.

"Well," Carsten replied, "Phoenix is gettin' a little too big for me."

"Amen to that," Fleur said, and kissed him on the cheek.

As Carsten left the courthouse, he noticed Ramona loitering by the steps. He walked down toward her.

"I misjudged you," Ramona said as they shook hands. "You truly are worthy of your reputation, Quaker McNeil."

"Thanks," Carsten replied with a weak smile. "I appreciate that. What are you gonna do now?"

"Take some time to lick my wounds," she replied. "I got plenty from my shares of yours and Garrett's bounties."

"So we're even now?" Carsten asked.

"I get paid on handover, not conviction," Ramona said with a faint smile. "So we have concluded the business between us. It ain't often I get to have this kind of friendly chat with my bounties."

"I was wanted, and you had a job to do," Carsten replied. "No hard feelin's."

"Until we meet again," Ramona said as she walked away.

"Next time, I'll definitely be on the right side of the law," Carsten said.

"I'm countin' on it," Ramona said as she turned around. "Adiós."

Carsten watched her walk away.

"So, what do we do now?" Attie asked.

"Take the next train back to Prescott," Carsten said. "Then go home. I don't know 'bout y'all, but I could use a couple days to put my feet up."

Epilogue
All's Well That
Ends Well

Carsten said nothing as he rode down the trail toward the McNeil Ranch.

"Hey," Fleur said as she walked her horse parallel to his. "Penny for your thoughts?"

"I'm just thinkin' 'bout what my folks are gonna say," Carsten replied without making eye contact. "I bet it broke Pa when he heard I was wanted by the law. Do you reckon the news has reached home?"

Morris rode over and patted his brother on the shoulder. "I wouldn't worry 'bout it," he replied. "I told him not to judge you till I came back."

"That's comfortin'," Carsten said.

"You'll be fine," Attie said. "This story woulda made the papers all across the territory, I reckon. We got our copy which we can show them." She handed him a rolled-up copy of the *Phoenix Herald*.

"Even if they ain't happy," Morris added, "just give 'em time."

The sun set as they approached the yard. Davey and Mike were sitting on the porch with Vince.

"They're back!" Davey yelled with enthusiasm as they dismounted. "Mrs. McNeil!"

As Attie ran into Davey's arms, Cassie ran outside. "You're back!" she said as she embraced Morris. "I've been worried sick!" She turned to Carsten.

Vince hobbled toward them. Both parents had stern expressions. Carsten unfolded the newspaper and showed them the front page.

"Deputy McNeil exonerated of all charges," Vince read the headline aloud.

Carsten noticed their expressions soften. "It means I'm no longer wanted. I'm sorry I put you through all that. It's a long story, and it ain't one I wanna tell without a drink in my hand. Morris and Attie told me it disappointed you when the posse came knockin'."

"We weren't disappointed," Vince said. "We were just afraid we'd never see you again. That you'd be living the rest of your days as an outlaw. Sounds like you and Fleur had quite an adventure."

"We certainly did," Fleur said.

"You must be hungry," Cassie said. "Dinner's nearly ready. Any idea about what you're gonna be doin'?"

"I'm gonna be sworn in as a full-on marshal soon," Carsten said. "I'll keep my office in Prescott while puttin' down a payment on a new house with the salary I'm gettin'. Not to mention my share of the bounty from the scofflaws I brought in. Spent a fair bit of that already, though."

"Well, why don't we head inside, and you can tell us about this little misadventure?" Cassie asked.

"I'll be in directly," Carsten said. "But there's somethin' else I gotta get off my chest." He turned to Fleur. "I picked up a little somethin' in town, and I figured this would be the best time to bring it up."

"Bring what up?" Fleur asked with a smile.

Carsten reached into his pocket and bent down on one knee in front of Fleur. Holding out his hand, he revealed a pair of rings. "Fleur Carpentier," he said, "will you marry me?"

She gasped. Tears welled in her eyes. "Yes," she said, extending her hand.

Carsten placed the ring on her finger. He stood up and embraced her as the rest of the family applauded.

Carsten blinked for a moment.

"This adventure I followed you on was even bigger than the last one," she said. "We've both been in gunfights. I think I could get used to that."

Carsten glanced at his brother, who shrugged. Attie gave him the thumbs up.

"I don't doubt it," he said after a pause.

The End

Thanks for taking the time to read this story. A positive review on Amazon would be appreciated.